Norse Mythology

A Timeless Journey where the Ancient Myths of the North Come to Life. Meet the Heroes, Gods, and Mythological Creatures that have Shaped a Unique and Fascinating Culture

Einar Lindberg

© Copyright 2023 by Einar Lindberg – Inkwell House Press
All rights reserved.
This document is geared towards providing exact and reliable information with regards to the topic and issue covered. The publication is sold with the idea that the publisher is not required to render accounting, officially permitted, or otherwise, qualified services. If advice is necessary, legal or professional, a practiced individual in the profession should be ordered.
- From a Declaration of Principles which was accepted and approved equally by a Committee of the American Bar Association and a Committee of Publishers and Associations.
In no way is it legal to reproduce, duplicate, or transmit any part of this document in either electronic means or in printed format. Recording of this publication is strictly prohibited and any storage of this document is not allowed unless with written permission from the publisher. All rights reserved.
The information provided herein is stated to be truthful and consistent, in that any liability, in terms of inattention or otherwise, by any usage or abuse of any policies, processes, or directions contained within is the solitary and utter responsibility of the recipient reader. Under no circumstances will any legal responsibility or blame be held against the publisher for any reparation, damages, or monetary loss due to the information herein, either directly or indirectly.
Respective authors own all copyrights not held by the publisher.
The information herein is offered for informational purposes solely, and is universal as so. The presentation of the information is without contract or any type of guarantee assurance. The trademarks that are used are without any consent, and the publication of the trademark is without permission or backing by the trademark owner. All trademarks and brands within this book are for clarifying purposes only and are the owned by the owners themselves, not affiliated with this document.

EXTRA BONUS

RUNES IN NORSE PAGANISM

-

ANCIENT PATHWAYS IN CONTEMPORARY PRACTICES

GO TO THE END OF THE BOOK AND SCAN THE QR CODE

Summary

INTRODUCTION	- 6 -
CHAPTER 1	- 7 -
CHAPTER 2	- 12 -
CHAPTER 3	- 18 -
CHAPTER 4	- 27 -
CHAPTER 5	- 35 -
CHAPTER 6	- 88 -
CHAPTER 7	- 103 -
CHAPTER 8	- 109 -
CHAPTER 9	- 114 -
CONCLUSION	- 121 -
DEAR READER…	- 123 -

INTRODUCTION

Imagine for a moment standing on the misty shores of Scandinavia, where the sea stretches as far as the eye can see and the fjords carve deep into the land like scars of ancient battles. Feel the chill of the air and the promise of adventure that tingles your skin. This is where we shall begin our journey into the mesmerizing realm of Norse mythology—a tapestry of tales that has gripped the imagination of humanity for countless generations. This is not merely a world of gods and mortals; it is a living, breathing epic that finds its roots in the fog-laden landscapes of the Vikings.

In this odyssey of gods and heroes, we encounter figures of monumental influence, such as Odin, the Allfather, whose wisdom knows no bounds; Thor, whose hammer quakes even the heavens; and Freyja, the embodiment of love and beauty, but also of fierce combat. They share the stage with a fascinating ensemble of giants, dwarves, and elves, each contributing their own thread to the intricately woven fabric of myths and legends.

And what stories these are! Tales replete with valor, betrayal, love lost and found, and destinies grander than the most towering fjords. These are not mere fables, mind you, but windows into the psyche of ancient peoples, offering us irreplaceable insights into their perceptions of life, death, and the labyrinthine nature of existence itself.

We will go beyond the lore to delve into the cradle from which these tales emerged, exploring not just the divine exploits but also the earthly settings—the societal norms, the cultural beliefs, the very essence of life as it was understood by our Norse ancestors. Imagine holding a Viking sword, smelling the salt and seaweed in the shipyards, or hearing the poetic verses sung in smoky mead halls. All of these serve as layers, adding depth and richness to the stories we explore.

So, whether you are a seasoned scholar of myths, a lover of history, or simply someone drawn like a moth to the flame of ancient stories, I invite you to join me. Let's unfurl the sails, seize the oars, and journey through the sea of time to revisit these enchanting tales. Tales that were told beneath the flicker of the Northern Lights, spoken in the glow of roaring hearths, and are now ready to captivate your imagination. A world of fascinating stories awaits you; let's step aboard and begin our expedition!

CHAPTER 1
The Ancient Roots of Norse Mythology

Vikings Origins
Picture yourself standing on the edge of a wind-whipped cliff overlooking the frigid Nordic waters. In the distance, you see a dragon-headed longship slicing through the waves, propelled by the sinewy arms of rowers. What images flood your mind when you think of Vikings? Is it a horde of savage plunderers descending on a helpless village? If so, let's set sail on a journey through time to break away from the chains of these stereotypes and discover the real tapestry of Viking life, one that is woven with strands far more complex and colorful.

You see, Vikings were not just warriors; they were also farmers tilling the cold soil, fishermen casting nets into the bounty-filled sea, and craftsmen carving intricate patterns onto pieces of wood and metal. These were the threads of everyday existence, contributing to a vibrant, albeit often misunderstood, social fabric.

Ah, the term "Viking." The word itself unfurls like a sail caught in the wind. It comes from the Old Norse word "vikingr," which might translate to "pirate" or "raider." Yet, it's worth noting that the term was originally more of an action than an identity. In the vernacular of the times, to "go Viking" was to embark on sea voyages that could be for trade or, yes, sometimes for raiding. Many of these were seasonal journeys, fueled by the need to sustain their communities through harsh winters or to explore unknown horizons. It was a chosen way of life, not a label stamped from birth.

In the parchment pages of ancient records, the term "Viking" is scarcely found. Instead, these seafaring people were referred to by other names such as "Normanni," the men of the north, or "Pagani," a nod to their polytheistic beliefs. Even "Dani," identifying them as Danes, was commonly used. The word "Viking" only spread its wings during the 11th century, long after many of the initial sea voyages had been etched into the annals of history.

And let us not forget their impact on European culture and economy. Far from being mere marauders, they were also connectors of worlds, traders of goods, and sharers of ideas. The routes they opened linked isolated communities, infused different cultures with fresh perspectives, and enabled the exchange of goods from far-off lands. The Viking longship was not merely a vehicle of war; it was a vessel of civilization, floating on currents of cultural and economic exchange.

Viking Raids in England
Envision the year 865, as autumn leaves fall gently onto the meandering paths of Anglo-Saxon England. Suddenly, the skies darken and the wind carries whispers of impending doom. Longships emerge from the misty North Sea. The

dreaded Vikings have arrived! Their reputation precedes them: mighty warriors from the frigid lands of Scandinavia, known for their audacious raids and conquests. The very name sends shivers down the spines of villagers, monks, and nobles alike.

Yet, in the annals of history, the Vikings' story unfolds with layers as intricate as the knotwork on their shields. Why did these seafaring Scandinavians venture so far from their fjord-lined homelands? Historians still weave theories as they comb through the loom of time. Was it the search for fertile land, driven by the unyielding harshness of their native climate? Or were they enticed by stories from traders and merchants about distant lands teeming with untold resources? This question, a riddle wrapped in the fog of the ages, continues to intrigue scholars to this day.

Once they unfurled their sails and set course across the turbulent waters, the Vikings were not mere plunderers. They were also empire-builders. They left their mark from the rocky coasts of Scotland and Ireland to the heartlands of France. Islands like Orkney in Scotland, the Hebrides, and the Shetlands became Norse strongholds. Meanwhile, in the fragmented lands of the Frankish Kingdom, they carved out territories for themselves, exploiting the political fissures that fractured the realm.

But let us not forget England, where the Vikings carved a saga that still reverberates through the annals of history. Led by the warrior brothers Ivar and Halfdan, their ships appeared like apparitions on the English coasts. Kingdom after kingdom fell to their swords and spears, save for one resilient realm: Wessex. Here emerges a hero, Alfred the Great, a name that still resonates like a battle cry. His military ingenuity and fortifications became the ramparts upon which Viking advances would break.

For nearly a century, the land was a tapestry of contrasting realms: the north and midlands under Norse rule, and the south under the steadfast governance of Wessex. Erik Bloodaxe, a name that could only belong to a Viking, was the last Norse king to wield power over English soil. Yet even after his expulsion in 954, the Viking saga did not end. Their influence extended beyond the English Channel, into lands as distant as Russia, Ukraine, and Normandy—the very place where Rollo, the great-great-grandfather of William the Conqueror, laid his roots.

Other Viking Settlements

The Vikings, these Norse wanderers of yore conjure images that dart like comets across the sky of our imaginations. They were not merely seafaring invaders; rather, they were people with complex aspirations. Imagine setting foot on English soil after a perilous raid, only to become so bewitched by its climate and soil that you signal for your family to follow. They were not just warriors, but also colonizers and farmers. These men and women were molded by an intricate alloy of motivations: the allure of wealth, the quest for prestige, and an almost mystical belief that their odysseys had received divine approval.

Consider the incalculable variables that propel us on any given venture. Now amplify that by a Nordic sense of destiny, a yearning for freedom, and an untamed ambition to influence global trade and politics. It is against this complex backdrop of human desire and daring that we must paint the broad strokes of Viking settlements.

The Faroe Islands

Let us journey to the Faroe Islands, a remote archipelago touched by Viking curiosity. As historical records penned by an Irish monk in 825 suggest, these isles once offered solitude to monks before being claimed by these Norse arrivals. In poetic simplicity, the Vikings named these islands "Fareyjar," or "Sheep Islands," after their abundant ovine inhabitants. Bereft of timber, these resolute settlers fashioned homes from rocks and turf, their daily lives beating in tune with the rhythms of the sea and livestock rearing.

Iceland

As we turn our gaze toward Iceland, we find that it wasn't love at first sight for the Vikings. The island's chilly winters were discouraging enough to hold off immediate settlement. But nearly a decade later, imagine a flotilla of settlers—predominantly Norwegians—drawn by the promise of freedom from the oppressive rule of King Harald Fairhair. They decided to make this remote island their home, thus penning a new chapter in the annals of Viking settlements.

Greenland

Greenland, an icy tableau that calls to mind the intrepid Vikings who once made it their home. Imagine the audacious Erik the Red, with his mane and beard as fiery red as a Nordic sunset. He was no stranger to controversy, having been exiled from Norway for reasons encapsulated by the phrase "some killings." With such a past, Erik knew that his new land would require rebranding. What better way to attract settlers than to name this ice-cloaked expanse "Greenland"? A name that seemed almost paradoxical, given that it was far colder than Iceland.

So, how did they even reach this misnamed 'Greenland'? Picture it: The year is 985, and 25 Viking ships leave the shores of Iceland, their sails filled with hopes and dreams. Now imagine the suspense and heartbreak when only 14 of these vessels reach Greenland. The others? Either swallowed by the sea or wrecked beyond repair. Yet, the survivors were undeterred. They established their new lives on the eastern and western coasts of Greenland. The native Inuit, perhaps wisely, chose to reside farther north, avoiding direct conflict with these newcomers.

The climate in Greenland presented its own narrative of struggles. While pockets of the coast were suitable for livestock, traditional farming was virtually impossible. Imagine a lifestyle adapted to these inhospitable conditions, where the sea was not merely a body of water but also a vital resource. For sustenance and trade, the Vikings relied on what the icy waters could offer: whales, seals, walruses. These were not mere animals; they were maritime treasures that commanded high prices in the markets of their time.

Yet, as we turn the final page of this Greenlandic Viking saga, we find nothing. A gaping void in history exists. Between the 15th and 17th centuries, the Viking settlers in Greenland seemed to vanish into the thin, Arctic air. Was it climate change, disease, or conflict with the native Inuit? Despite modern efforts to decipher this riddle, we remain in the realm of speculation. Like a tale told by the Northern Lights, the story of the Vikings in Greenland beckons us: elusive and hypnotic, urging us to keep pondering, questioning, and marveling at the resilience and enigma of human history.

Russia and France

The sinuous rivers of Russia served as watery highways for Viking longboats; this was not mere exploration but a saga of foundation and dominion. From the 9th to the 16th century, Vikings gave rise to the Rurikid dynasty in what became known as Rus. Although the land was largely inhabited by Slavs, the helm of power was grasped by these Scandinavian conquerors.

Now, let's turn our gaze to France, where the longboats first appeared in the tumultuous year of 799. In a Frankish kingdom rife with political turmoil, these seafaring Norsemen gained significant footholds. By 885, they were at the very doorstep of Paris, ready to etch their saga into the heart of Europe. However, the Carolingian Empire rose as a colossal barricade, thwarting the Viking advance. The influence they managed to exert in France could never match their sweeping victories in England, Ireland, or Scotland. Yet their legacy persists—visible in two quaint settlements along the Seine River, founded in the 10th century.

Further east, the Viking tapestry takes on a different hue. Eastern Europe saw Viking incursions that were noticeably less violent. No kingdoms were carved out by sword and axe here. However, the Vikings who did venture into this territory integrated so seamlessly with the Slavic inhabitants that they simply came to be known as "the Rus."

As the sunset on the 11th century, so too did the Viking era. The leadership gradually faded, making room for new alliances and territories. Norway, Sweden, and Denmark coalesced into what would later evolve into distinct kingdoms. This metamorphosis occurred through adventures, explorations, and, in Denmark's case, the strategic enlistment of gallant young men into its military ranks. The last echoes of Viking valor resonated in Olaf II Haraldson's crowning as King of Norway in 1015, signaling not just the end of one monumental epoch but also the dawn of a new European chapter.

Who Were the Vikings?

Along the seashores of Scandinavia, where audacious men prepare their vessels, you've probably heard of their exploits along the British coastline. But did you know that these Scandinavian adventurers actually set foot in North America a full 500 years before Christopher Columbus ever sailed across the Atlantic? Quite astonishing, isn't it?

When you think about maritime prowess, the Vikings epitomize it. They were the first significant naval power, crafting longboats meticulously designed for swift attacks and raids. These boats were so cherished and integral to their lives that they often chose to be buried with them. Should you wish to lay eyes on such vessels, you can: Norway's museums are home to these historic longboats. Furthermore, just a few years ago, in 2018, an entire graveyard of Viking ships was discovered. They had been buried on land, serving as a silent testament to their significance in Viking culture.

Now, if you've been imagining the Vikings as merciless raiders, you're only scratching the surface of their story. These men not only embarked on expeditions but also crafted laws and developed runic writing systems. They explored and traded, impacting commerce in ways still tangible today. Turn your gaze toward Eastern Europe, and you'll find that the Vikings were instrumental in shaping what later became known as Russia. They were absorbed, assimilated, and they profoundly influenced the land.

So how do we know all this? Much of what we understand about the Vikings has been passed down through generations, often orally. However, they also left physical records: runestones. Carved with intricate markings, these stones captured the tales and beliefs of the time and were later translated into Latin after the Vikings' descendants found themselves under Roman rule. Because of this, today we have an intimate window into the social fabric and customs of the Viking or Norse kingdoms.

But the image of Vikings as fearsome seafarers is just one facet of a much broader mosaic. Imagine the vast, serene landscapes of Scandinavia, a terrain dotted not only with longboats but also with farming communities. Most Viking homesteads were intricately designed for purposes beyond raiding: they were cultivated to produce food and to act as sanctuaries during times of famine or illness.

When the British Isles fortified their coastlines with sea forts, effectively ending the golden age of Viking raids, what did our adventurous Norsemen do? They adapted, naturally, turning their seafaring expertise toward trade. Can you believe they ventured as far as the bustling markets of Baghdad? Their sails caught winds that filled not only their sails but also the annals of history.

CHAPTER 2
Norse Culture

The spellbinding world of Norse culture and mythology is as alive and palpable today as the frosty winds sweeping through the fjords of Scandinavia. Indeed, anyone with a sense of adventure can tour sacred sites in Norway, Sweden, or Denmark. If you prefer the comfort of your own home, an impressive array of websites and social media platforms are available at your fingertips, inviting you to delve into this fascinating tradition. But let's pause and examine how our collective understanding of Norse gods and myths has evolved over the centuries.

Life in the Viking Age

The Viking Age is often caricatured as a period rife with violence and plunder. Yet, this paints an incomplete picture. The majority of Vikings led rather pastoral lives, diligently tending to their farms and livestock. Despite their reputation as fearsome warriors, many lived in rural communities and were as proficient with the plow as they were with the sword.

Viking society had its intricacies, marked by clearly defined roles and responsibilities for men and women. While men were engaged in tasks beyond the household boundaries—such as farming, fishing, and livestock tending—women were the domestic architects, spinning the fabric of daily life through cooking and clothing creation. Yet, come harvest time, a sense of communal spirit prevailed. Even children lent their hands to the efforts, and the dividing lines of labor blurred for the collective good.

Slave labor bore the weight of the more physically grueling tasks, such as pulling heavy plows, erecting buildings, or spreading manure on fields. These slaves were often prisoners captured in Viking raids or skirmishes.

Craftsmanship had its place within these farmsteads. While blacksmithing was often performed on an as-needed basis in rural settings, urban areas had their specialists. Payment for their expertise would typically be in the form of food or other barter.

Life for the Vikings was not for the faint-hearted. Farm work was harsh and labor-intensive, devoid of the comforts of modern machinery. And then there were the winters—imagine a season so merciless that it could bring even the most robust Viking to his knees. Natural disasters, raids, and famines often disrupted agricultural routines, leaving families in precarious situations, struggling to make it through the long, unforgiving cold.

Health was another relentless adversary. Diseases and famine plagued these communities. It's startling to realize that nearly one-third of Viking children did not live to see adulthood, a grim statistic etched in the annals of archaeology.

But let's not forget their ingenuity in overcoming the geographical challenges they faced. Horses were their primary means of land transport, yet wagons and carts were also used for heavier duties. In winter, the landscape transformed into a snowy labyrinth navigable only by ingeniously crafted skis and sleds.

The challenges were immense, yet this makes the Vikings' accomplishments all the more astonishing. From these gritty, everyday struggles arose a culture so rich, so deeply entwined with the divine and the mystical, that it continues to enrapture our imaginations today. A truly incredible journey through time, don't you think?

Social Classes

Viking society was a structure woven with strict threads of social hierarchy. Step into this vivid panorama, and you'll find three principal layers: slaves, free men, and earls. Each of these classes carried its own set of conditions, opportunities, and grim realities. Shall we delve deeper?

Consider, for a moment, the plight of Viking slaves, the individuals treading the very bottom of the social pyramid. Their descent into slavery could occur through various pathways. Captured in the throes of battle or the aftermath of a raid, some found themselves enslaved, their lives spared in exchange for freedom—a bargain from the Viking perspective. Others were simply unfortunate enough to be born into this state, as children of slaves inevitably inherited the shackles of their parents. Then there were those who voluntarily gave up their freedom, a desperate move to escape the clutches of bankruptcy. They traded autonomy for the basest of necessities: food, clothing, and shelter. It's crucial to understand that, as harsh as the life of a Viking slave was, it also served as a grim social safety net of sorts. For the destitute, it provided a way to stave off hunger and evade the predatory reach of creditors. Once enslaved, most were put to work on farms. However, their owners could also thrust them into the bustling European slave trade. Some accounts even tell of slaves being sacrificed upon the death of their master, a chilling testament to the belief that their servitude persisted even in the afterlife. For Viking slaves, prospects were far from uplifting.

While it's easy to assume their lives were miserable, let's not rush to judgment. Unlike in some other societies, where slavery was brutally oppressive, slaves in Viking society were generally treated decently. They were offered a place to live and provided with safety.

Next, consider the free men, the backbone of Viking society. This large and diverse group included everyone from prosperous landowners to modest farmers who tilled another's land in exchange for a small plot to call their own. Merchants, craftsmen, and warriors also fit into this category. When envisioning a Viking raider, it is these free men who most often come to mind. It's fascinating to think that Viking expeditions were largely undertaken by these young men, primarily the younger sons who inherited less and had fewer ties to their homeland. Fueled by ambition and protected by law, these young adventurers set out to find silver, land, and a brighter future in far-off colonies and settlements.

And finally, perched atop this complex social hierarchy were the jarls, or earls, as we might more commonly call them today. These men controlled vast tracts of land where their subjects toiled. Far from being merely exploitative, they were responsible for the well-being of their subjects, for resolving disputes, and for maintaining the law. In return, they were obliged to pay taxes to the overarching kings who ruled these lands. Power in this tier was often accrued through military conquest—be it raids, territorial expansions, or other means.

Initially, these were chieftains who had amassed wealth through the age-old Viking practices of raiding and plundering. As time wore on, their role evolved. By the twilight years of the Viking Age, these jarls had metamorphosed into figures resembling medieval aristocrats, subordinates to a king, with the power to amass lands as they saw fit.

Viking Politics

Viking politics constituted a realm where the intricate dance of power and loyalty played out on a brutal yet captivating stage. Within the microcosm of Viking society, political control was largely vested in chieftains and clan leaders. These individuals were not merely rulers; they were figures of awe, commanding small but fierce bands of warriors. To rise to such a position, a chieftain had to exhibit an array of virtues: fearlessness, generosity, and an unblemished record of victories in battle.

You may wonder how these chieftains maintained their status. The answer lies in a cunning blend of valor and patronage. Successful forays into battle yielded riches, which served multiple purposes. They could be distributed to followers, not in the form of coins—currency for a later time—but as more tangible treasures: silver, gold, and arm rings that ranged from austere to ornate. Even plots of land became tokens of favor, vital for anyone in Viking society aiming for success.

What, then, would a chieftain do with this accumulated wealth? The answer can be found in the grand feasts, occasions often imbued with religious undertones. These banquets were not merely about satiating hunger or enjoying revelry; they served as critical social contracts. The chieftain's generosity exacted a price: unwavering loyalty. This loyalty transcended mere economic incentives and touched the very fabric of Viking honor. Many a warrior considered it the highest accolade to die in battle, shoulder to shoulder with their leader. For them, the allure was not just wealth but also a profound sense of belonging and honor, which a wise chieftain could astutely offer.

Commerce

Now let's turn our attention from the battlefields and feasting halls to the bustling marketplaces and harbors. Vikings were master traders, their reach extending even to far-off lands like Baghdad and Asia. Picture this: amid the fjords and rugged landscapes, trade towns sprang up as bustling centers of craft specialization—be it jewelry-making, blacksmithing, or antler work—primarily geared for export. These towns were far more than mere marketplaces; they served as conduits connecting the isolated Scandinavian world to the complex web of Eurasian trade routes. In doing so, these towns ushered in an era of commerce that would come to define the Vikings as much as their raids and sagas did.

Gender Roles in the Viking Age

Let us now explore the intimate sphere of the Viking household, a realm governed by a strict but deeply ingrained set of gender roles. In these homes, men were the warriors and farmers, serving as the backbone of Viking societal structure. They were lauded and immortalized through epic tales—sagas that rolled off the tongues of skalds, or Viking poets. Women, by contrast, were the custodians of the domestic sphere, responsible for home and hearth. While their contributions were invaluable, they were not typically heralded in song or story. Their form of heroism, if it may be termed as such, was celebrated in a quieter manner, within the walls of their homes and in the eyes of their communities.

Now let's consider the institution of marriage, a domain where women had limited autonomy. Marriage proposals were solely the prerogative of men, and it was the bride's family that deliberated on the merits of the union. Additionally, a double standard existed regarding marital fidelity. A man discovered to be unfaithful faced penalties, but these were far less severe than those meted out to an adulterous woman. For such women, the consequences could be as dire as death at the hands of their own husbands. While men—especially those of higher status, such as warlords and kings—could possess multiple wives and concubines, women were expected to maintain unwavering loyalty to their spouses.

However, it would be inaccurate to consider Viking women as entirely powerless; they did have some rights. For example, a woman could seek a divorce if she found herself in a dysfunctional marriage. If she managed to prove her husband's misconduct, she was entitled to compensation, providing her a measure of financial independence post-divorce.

As for professions, here we encounter the glass ceiling of the Viking Age. Women were largely consigned to domestic roles. Tilling the land, wielding political power, voicing opinions in assemblies, fighting as warriors, and even the act of leaving their homeland for adventure—these were pursuits almost exclusively reserved for men. There was, however, one intriguing exception: sorceresses. These women were believed to possess magical abilities capable of tipping the scales of battle. Nonetheless, even they were not commonly found on the battlefield; their role was more mystical than tactical.

Food, Clothing, Jewelry, and Weapons of the Viking Age

Let's now explore the domesticity of Viking life, where daily rituals ranged from the food on the table to the garments that clothed their bodies. Picture a Viking family gathering around a meal. What's on the menu? In the realm of Viking culinary arts, geography determined destiny. Depending on the Scandinavian region they inhabited, different resources were available. Yet, one food item remained a universal staple: barley. This grain was the essence of their bread-making, appearing in various forms such as loaves and buns. But its culinary versatility didn't end there; it also combined with other grains like oats, flax, and rye. Surprisingly, even pine bark sometimes found its way into their recipes.

Ah, the aroma of dairy! Cattle, sheep, and goats grazed on fertile lands, offering an abundance of milk, cheese, and butter. Given their proximity to the sprawling coastline, these people also had access to the bounty of the sea. Picture herring and cod sizzling on their hearths, maritime treasures gracing their tables. Their taste buds craved even more; the thrill of the hunt placed deer, rabbits, boars, and even seals and whales on their platters. Oils extracted from these animals served as culinary luxuries, used either for cooking or as decadent substitutes for butter.

Despite their fierce demeanor, these warriors also had more delicate palates. Their gardens produced cabbages, peas, beets, and beans, while their forests yielded a variety of wild fruits and berries. Strawberries, blackberries, pears, cherries, and hazelnuts—foods that nourished not just the body but also the soul. Indeed, these indomitable warriors understood the value of a balanced diet, a harmonious blend of flavors and nutrients.

Turning now to Viking attire, wool and flax served as shields against the biting cold. Women spun these fibers into threads and wove them into garments, a task that could be seen as a labor of love. Wealthier families had the luxury of purchasing ready-made fabrics, perhaps a testament to their social standing. Linen was prized for undergarments, its soft texture preferred against the skin. Fur, conversely, was a symbol of elegance, used to adorn cloaks and trim garments. While they had a fondness for color, the natural dyes they employed were often temporary, their vibrancy a transient beauty.

Viking life wasn't solely about practicality; it also had its flair and fashions. Jewelry served as more than mere ornamentation; it functioned as social currency, a wearable status symbol that could be bartered when necessary. Rings, necklaces, brooches, and amulets adorned their persons, featuring motifs like Thor's hammer and miniature thrones that reflected their beliefs and aspirations.

As we know, a Viking was seldom without a weapon. Swords epitomized martial elegance and were wielded only by the elite. Axes, on the other hand, were the utilitarian choice, simple in design but versatile in function. Spears, bows, and arrows completed the Viking armory, each weapon having a specific purpose, whether for throwing, thrusting, or causing general havoc. Let's dispel a myth: those horned helmets that have captured popular imagination are a fanciful invention. In reality, Viking helmets were practical, made of leather or iron, and devoid of ostentation.

CHAPTER 3
Norse Beliefs

Norse Mythology

There is a universe teeming with gods and giants, clashing in epic battles, their struggles propelling us toward the apocalyptic end of days. These myths served as the spiritual cornerstones for the people of Denmark, Sweden, Norway, and even the northern reaches of Germany. The landscapes may differ, but imagination knows no boundaries.

So, let's meet these gods who occupy the celestial stage of this mythical drama. There's Thor, a god of such fierce valor that his hammer seems an extension of his own indomitable will. Then we have Odin, the wise and complex god of both battle and poetry, a juxtaposition that only enriches his character. Don't forget Njord, the great bestower of wealth and fertile lands. Rest assured, these divine figures, along with their entourage—giants, elves, dwarfs, trolls, and even human warriors of legend—will be elaborated upon in intricate detail in the chapters to follow.

But the gods are not a monolithic group. They divide into two distinct families: the Æsir and the Vanir. Picture the Æsir as the gods of the sky, the aristocracy of the heavens, captained by none other than Odin, who also carries the honor of being the creator of humans. On the other side, we have the Vanir, the gods of the earth, the bringers of fertility and prosperity. Drama unfolded when these two divine clans found themselves in conflict, but wisdom prevailed. Recognizing that neither could vanquish the other, they formed an alliance against a common foe: the Giants. To solidify this newfound peace, some of the Vanir—Njord, Freyr, and Freyja—were even sent to Asgard, the stronghold of the Æsir, as hostages.

You may be intrigued to know that this elaborate system of myths didn't materialize out of thin air. These stories have roots in the beliefs of the Germanic-speaking peoples of the north. As some of these groups migrated to England and Scandinavia, their myths traveled with them. While many converted to Christianity, causing their original beliefs to wane, in Scandinavia these mythological stories held on tenaciously, particularly during the Viking era that spanned from around AD 750 to 1050. So here we are, immersed in the sumptuous universe of Norse mythology—a cosmos teeming with diverse beings, from gods to giants to elves and heroic humans. Each myth, each character offers a unique lens into the values and beliefs of the people who revered them. Even today, these tales hold an uncanny ability to captivate us, beckoning us to explore a world so different, yet so resonant with our own quests for meaning and adventure.

The Creation of the Cosmos
The world was believed to be divided into nine intricate and interconnected dimensions, all held together by Yggdrasil, the majestic tree of life. Consider Asgard, the abode of gods, and Vanaheim, the home of the Vanir. Don't overlook Midgard, where humans dwell, or the dark Niflheim, akin to the underworld. The way these realms capture our imagination is utterly captivating.

Let's venture back to the very beginning. Picture infinite emptiness—utter nothingness. Yet within this abyss, a realm of elemental fire known as Muspelheim comes into existence. The world is aflame, blindingly bright and scorchingly hot. Only the primordial beings born of this fire can endure its intensity. Imagine rivers with deadly flows turning into solid masses.
Now picture a stark contrast: Niflheim, the realm of elemental ice. Envision a world tormented by harsh winds, persistent rain, and biting cold. The chilling heart of this realm is a fountain named Hvergelmir, which gives rise to twelve rivers that snake their way through the abyss. It's like stepping into a haunting painting of a winter night.
At the confluence of these polar opposites stands Ginnungagap, an abyss, an eternal void that yawns between Muspelheim to the south and Niflheim to the north. A remarkable event occurs here: the fiery heat of Muspelheim meets the frosty chill of Niflheim, and from the ensuing meltwater, Ymir, the first frost giant, is born.

Ymir is an androgynous being with unique reproductive capabilities. On the night of his birth, Ymir begins to sweat, and from his sweat, new giants emerge. To sustain himself, Ymir drinks the milk of Audhumbla, a cow also born from the melting ice. She, in turn, finds sustenance by licking salty ice blocks. From these blocks, a man of great strength and beauty emerges: Buri, the progenitor of the Aesir gods.

Buri fathers Bor, who unites with Bestla—potentially a daughter of Ymir or, at the very least, a descendant of Bolthorn, also known as Boelthor. From this unprecedented union between a god and a giant, a trio of sons is born: Odin, Vili, and Ve. These three, with their dual lineage, will ultimately shape the destiny of the world. First on their agenda is a rather sinister plot to murder Ymir and subsequent generations of giants, beginning, no less, with their own maternal grandfather.

After slaying the great giant Ymir, Odin and his brothers had the foresight to lift the fallen giant's lifeless body from the sea of his own blood that flooded the infinite void. There, right between the fervent heat of Muspelheim and the icy gusts of Niflheim, they founded Earth. Ymir's flesh metamorphosed into the ground we tread upon, while his blood gave birth to the oceans. The mountains? Ah, those were his bones, transformed. Even the trees that grace our landscapes were once Ymir's hair.

Look upward and you'll find the Vault of Heavens—crafted from Ymir's very skull. Holding each corner of this cosmic canopy are four dwarves, appropriately named North, South, East, and West. If you ever wonder about the clouds that drift by, think of them as the remnants of Ymir's cognitive machinery—his brains, tossed into the sky like cosmic confetti.

Inside this celestial vault, the gods showcased their sense of cosmic aesthetics. They took embers and fire sparks that had escaped from Muspelheim and designated them to be our sun, moon, and stars. It was like setting a clockwork universe in motion, creating night and day, as well as winter and summer seasons. And the sun—oh, its radiant beams spurred the grass to grow.

The gods couldn't help but express their admiration for the cosmic artistry performed by Odin and his brothers. Together, they then embarked on constructing Asgard, a majestic dwelling poised just above Earth, or what the Norse called Midgard. Within this divine residence, each god established his own manor, as unique as the deity it housed. Ever wonder how gods commuted? They built Bifrost, a radiant bridge akin to our rainbows, stretching from Asgard to Midgard. The god Heimdall had the high honor of guarding this heavenly pathway.

But let's not forget the fortifications. Using Ymir's eyebrows—yes, his eyebrows—they crafted a protective barrier that shielded not just the gods but also the human inhabitants of Midgard from the lurking threats of giants.

You might think the gods would have overlooked the maggots wriggling in Ymir's decaying flesh. Ah, but not so! They were transformed into dwarves.

These subterranean beings were destined to reside within Earth's bowels, forever shielded from the sun's rays. Any dwarf touched by sunlight would petrify into stone. Dwarves were all male, lacking the means to procreate. To solve this puzzle, a pair of dwarf princes were divinely appointed, capable of molding new dwarves from soil and stones. And then came the humans—the Midgardians. Odin, along with either Hoenir and Lodur or Vili and Ve, depending on the version of the tale you subscribe to, stumbled upon two twisted tree trunks while wandering along a seashore. From these, they sculpted the first man and woman, breathing life into them and bestowing them with souls, reason, and even clothing. Ask and Embla were their names, and they were the progenitors of all humanity.

What a narrative we have here! A saga teeming with powerful gods and giants, of elemental realms fused together, of primal sacrifices and divine creations that set the stage for the world as we know it. Truly, the Norse myths are an inexhaustible well of stories, characters, and lessons that continue to intrigue and inspire us—carved into the very bones and sinews of human imagination.

Valhalla

Valhalla—the very utterance of the name conjures images of grandiosity, heroism, and an eternity of glory. Derived from the Old Norse "Valhöll," this legendary hall is a palace of myths, a place where the bravest of warriors find their eternal rest. Picture a majestic hall situated within the realms of Asgard, the celestial home of the Aesir gods. Odin, the chief among these gods, presides over this hall. But he is not alone; rather, he is surrounded by a cadre of valiant warriors who, in their afterlife, engage in a never-ending celebration of their bravery.

Imagine a lavish, unending banquet graced by these heroes of lore. They relive their most gallant battles, and they are not alone in this grand festivity. The radiant Valkyries, those ethereal maidens, attend to them, filling their cups with mead and readying them for their ultimate test—the cataclysmic event known as Ragnarök. For these fallen warriors, Valhalla is not merely a place; it is the epitome of honor, a prize for their courage and indomitable spirit. In essence, if you were a warrior who lived and breathed valor, Valhalla would be your eternal abode.

The Importance of Valhalla in Norse Mythology

Let's delve deeper into the role this fabled hall plays in Norse belief. For the Nordic peoples, the gods were not distant celestial beings; they were interwoven with the very fabric of daily life. Rituals and sacrifices were frequent, aimed at winning the gods' favor for success in war, bountiful harvests, and even fertility. Even elements of nature—water, mountains, and yes, even rocks—were held in profound, almost reverential regard.

This veneration of Valhalla and Odin exerted a powerful influence on the psychology of Viking warriors. These men, hardened by battle, did not fear death; rather, they embraced it as an audition for an even greater spectacle in the afterlife. Each swing of their sword, each battle cry, served as an offering, a performance intended to capture Odin's attention and earn them a seat in the divine hall.

Ah, the notion of dying of old age was not merely unfortunate for a Viking; it was considered a shame, a missed opportunity. Even the elderly, with stiff joints and gray beards, yearned for battle. Because, you see, even in their twilight years, battle offered them a final chance—a chance to impress Odin and secure a place in the eternal glory of Valhalla.

Viking Spirituality

Viking spirituality, a realm in which the mind, soul, and gods interact, represented a dual experience in the ancient Norse religion: rituals on one hand and mystical knowledge on the other. This system was designed not merely for the act of worship but also to explore profound questions—what is the universe, and what is our role within it? While time may have eroded the finer details of how exactly the Vikings worshipped their gods, one thing remains crystal clear: these deities commanded both respect and love, fulfilling the Vikings' spiritual, psychological, and social needs in an extraordinary manner.

One of the most celebrated ceremonies among these Nordic people was the "blot," a type of sacramental offering usually made in temples or special sanctified locations known as "blot houses." Human sacrifices, sometimes involving enemy rulers or noblemen, were offered to Odin. However, it wasn't just humans who were sacrificed. Animals, particularly those representing specific gods, also played a role in this complex ritual. For instance, Freyr, the god associated with fertility, was often venerated through the sacrifice of a boar. These sacrifices were not mere acts of devotion; they served a deeper purpose.

When religious practitioners consumed the animals during the blot, it was viewed as a form of spiritual communion, a way to connect more profoundly with the gods. Intriguingly, the Vikings believed that through these sacrifices, they were sending gifts upward to the gods as tokens of gratitude for earthly blessings and as gestures to maintain cosmic balance.

Let's clarify something: the Norse gods were not considered to be all-powerful or perfect. Understanding this is crucial, especially when considering how the Vikings transitioned to Christianity—a change that was neither rapid nor sudden, but slow and calculated. The challenge for early Christian missionaries was not simply introducing a new faith. Rather, the real task lay in persuading the Norsemen to abandon their polytheistic traditions and incorporate exclusively Christian elements into their lives.

Such a transformation could not be limited to religion alone; it was intrinsically linked to broader cultural shifts. As the Vikings increasingly adopted Christian practices, their governance evolved from tribal chieftaincies to more centralized monarchies. They embraced the Latin alphabet, altering their entire cultural outlook toward what could be described as a "Europeanization" process. Therefore, the adoption of Christianity was not simply an act of swapping gods; it was an evolution—a revolution—that spanned religious, social, and even political dimensions.

Norse Shamanism

While shamanism might be a term commonly associated with various cultures, the Norse version had its own unique nuances. Most notably, the leading figures in Norse shamanism were typically women. This is not to say that men were entirely absent from the shamanic scene; rather, they were present but played specialized roles, often aligning themselves with specific gods to assist their compatriots on the battlefield.

Let's delve a bit deeper. The roles of male and female shamans diverged quite significantly. Men were oriented toward warfare, invoking the powers of gods to aid in combat. On the other hand, female shamans focused on activities that were less confrontational but no less crucial. They assumed the responsibility of safeguarding the tribe's well-being, tapping into ethereal realms, orchestrating divination and healing, and channeling spiritual energies to ensure successful hunting and farming.

Norse Totemism

Another fascinating aspect of this spiritual landscape was the practice of totemism, a system in which humans and spiritual beings—in the form of animals or plants—shared an extraordinary, intimate connection. Among the Norse tribes, this manifested primarily through two potent forces. First, there were the Fylgjur, or animal spiritual guides, said to offer guidance and protection. Next, there were the patron animals that warriors would summon in the heat of battle, creatures both mythical and mighty. These totemic beliefs were not mere superstitions; they were considered essential channels that provided both individual and collective protection and guidance.

Magic and runes

The enigmatic world of runes offers a fascinating journey into the magical and mystical. The word "rune" itself, derived from Old Norse, encapsulates the essence of its meaning: "holding a secret". It's as if the term beckons us to unlock the hidden forces dormant within each inscribed symbol.

Let's not underestimate the gravity of this art form; it was far from a trivial pursuit. Even Odin, the Allfather and the most potent and wise of the Norse gods, had to pay a steep price to acquire the arcane wisdom that runes offered. Picture him hanging from the world tree Yggdrasil, his body pierced by a spear, forgoing food for nine agonizing days, and even sacrificing an eye. Odin's quest serves as a potent reminder that the path to mastering runes was perilous and required a high toll.

Once mastered, the runes could perform astonishing feats. From manipulating the weather to revealing the intricacies of destiny or enhancing personal attributes, their applications spanned both the practical and the sublime. Consider rune casting, a captivating ritual in which rune counters, often carved from bone or wood, were cast to seek answers from an oracle. The arrangement of these counters could then be interpreted by a seer, providing a glimpse into the future.

But runes were not solely about divination or manipulating external forces. They also had considerable healing properties. Take, for example, Egil's Saga, where the hero Egil uses runes to reverse a curse inflicted on a young girl by a sorceress. Placing specially inscribed runes under the girl's pillow led to her miraculous recovery. This episode illustrates that runes were versatile tools, neither inherently good nor evil, but mediums that channeled the will of the practitioner.

Would you believe that there are three different runic alphabets, each with its own unique timeline and geographical scope? The eldest among them is the Elder Futhark, which dates as far back as the first century C.E. and boasts 24 distinct characters. It remained in use until roughly 800 C.E. Subsequently, the Younger Futhark evolved, streamlined to 16 characters and closely associated with the Viking Age. Over time, it underwent transformation, adopting Latinized forms and earning the title "Medieval Futhark." Meanwhile, across the North Sea, the Anglo-Saxon Futhorc flourished, featuring its own set of 33 characters.

As time progressed and the influence of Christianity spread through Norse lands, an intriguing fusion began to take shape. Runic symbols were amalgamated with Christian ones, a synthesis that paradoxically contributed to the decline of pure runic practices as the church sought to ban them. However, runes never vanished entirely. After lying dormant for centuries, they have experienced a resurgence in modern times, a testament to their enduring appeal and influence.

Viking Magical Practices & Beliefs

For the ancient Norse and Germanic tribes, magic was not an act of altering reality but a way to harmonize with the natural laws of the cosmos. Indeed, during the Viking Age, magic was considered an essential means of acquiring wisdom. Surprisingly, vestiges of these beliefs endure even today.

Let's focus for a moment on the fundamental pillars underpinning Viking society. The Vikings were not merely concerned with battle strategies or territorial conquests. Instead, deeply ingrained in their consciousness were certain ideals—honor, faith in fate and divine powers, and a strong sense of community and family. These were not just abstract principles; they constituted the very fabric of their existence, guiding every action and decision made by these Norse warriors and their communities.

These foundational beliefs were not merely moral compasses but also detailed guides to living. The Vikings' perspective on life was deeply influenced by these principles, shaping their interactions with both the physical and metaphysical worlds. Magic, in this context, was not the antithesis of these values but rather an extension of them. It was a means of navigating the intricate pathways of fate, of reconciling with their gods, and of strengthening their familial and communal bonds.

Fate

Consider, for a moment, the overarching concept of fate, or "Urðr," as the Vikings would call it. This is not fate as many of us understand it today—as something we can fight against or change. Rather, this is an all-encompassing, almost deterministic fate that binds not just mortals but even gods. Imagine living your life with the understanding that no matter the choices you make, your ultimate destiny remains unaltered. The Norse did not view this as tragic but rather as a dimension of existence—amoral and indifferent, neither good nor evil. It simply was. The only beings that stood beyond this concept were the Norns, those mysterious figures who wove the threads of fate.

Magic of the Seidr

Now, let's explore the magic of seidr, the Norse's unique form of shamanism. What sets seidr apart is its scope—it could subtly influence fate. Picture a seidr practitioner chanting ancient verses, creating a magical space where a warrior fated to die might experience victory before succumbing. The art of seidr was not merely a ritualistic act; it was a complex dialogue with the universe, aiming to reveal prophecies, channel blessings, or even cast curses.

Their Sense of Self

To understand a Viking, one must comprehend how they viewed the "self." Modern psychology categorizes our sense of self into three components: the ego, id, and superego—or body, mind, and spirit, if you prefer. However, the Vikings had a more nuanced and interconnected view. Their understanding fragmented the self into various components, each with a specific role and purpose. Far from being merely a psychological construct, this vision was deeply embedded in their spirituality and daily life—a tradition that, surprisingly, resonates in the practices of today's Viking heritage.

CHAPTER 4
Yggdrasil and the Nine Realms

Yggdrasil

Yggdrasil, that colossal ash tree, serves as nothing less than the very cornerstone of existence itself. Often called the World Tree, it functions as the pivot, the axis, around which the entire cosmos rotates. Imagine roots extending into primordial worlds and branches reaching toward the skies as if to caress the divine.

Now, consider its three roots, which anchor the World Tree to distinct cosmic landscapes: Asgard, Jotunheim, and Niflheim. These roots do more than merely anchor Yggdrasil; they channel vital energies, mystical wisdom, and essential sustenance, maintaining the universe in its precarious balance.

Beneath the Asgard root, you'll discover Mimir's Well, a sanctuary of immeasurable wisdom. The second root reaches toward the Well of Urd in Jotunheim, where the Norns, awe-inspiring weavers of fate, etch runes into the fabric of existence. The third root extends to Niflheim, drawing its life-giving waters from the well of Hvergelmir.

The trunk of this magnificent tree is not just wood and bark; it's the Axis Mundi, a metaphysical conduit joining disparate worlds. It forms a passage through which gods, humans, and various other beings can traverse between realms. The trunk serves as a grand symphony of existence, uniting the physical and the spiritual, the mortal and the divine.

Above, the canopy extends its branches like the outstretched arms of a cosmic deity. An eagle resides there, symbolizing perhaps the pinnacle of life's ambitions and spiritual yearnings. A curious detail: a hawk named Vedrfolnir sits between the eagle's eyes, adding yet another layer to the enigma that is Yggdrasil.

Despite its majesty, Yggdrasil is not without its challenges. It serves as a sanctuary for creatures both benevolent and destructive. Four stags wander through its branches, nibbling at the leaves, while Nidhogg gnaws at its roots. These creatures signify universal truths of growth and decay, creation and destruction. They serve as reminders that everything, even this grand tree, is subject to the inexorable passage of time and cycles of life and death. Yggdrasil is more than a mere cosmic map; it's a living testament to the intricacies that govern all existence. Its role extends beyond functionality to deep symbolism. It represents balance, interconnectedness, the cyclic rhythm of life and death, and even an unquenchable thirst for knowledge and destiny.

Midgard (Earth)

Midgard, where humans reside, is not merely a realm isolated in space; it's integrated into a larger cosmological framework that encompasses nine intriguing worlds. Envision it as the beating heart of a universe, engaging in a cosmic dance with other realms. A vast ocean that encircles this realm, a body of water so immense that it harbors a creature of legend—Jörmungandr, the sea serpent. This awe-inspiring serpent encircles itself in an endless loop, holding its tail in its mouth, in a perpetual cycle symbolizing the eternal rhythm of life and death.

From Midgard, a radiant link known as the Bifröst bridge extends to Asgard, the celestial residence of gods. Guarded by the watchful Heimdall, this bridge is not just a physical connector. Consider it a metaphoric thread tying together the fates and destinies of gods and humans, marking an interdependent relationship as poetic as it is potent.

As you explore the various sagas and texts describing Midgard, you'll find something captivating: the landscape is a tableau of contrasts. Here, towering mountains meet expansive forests, and winding rivers flow into fertile plains. This diversity is not merely a geographical attribute; it serves as a mirror reflecting the intricate fabric of human experience, complete with its peaks and valleys, its bravery and apprehensions.

Now, let's contemplate Midgard's destiny for a moment. According to the prophetic narrative of Ragnarök, this realm will function as the stage for a battle so monumental it will encompass gods, giants, and an assortment of mythical beings. The earth trembling, the seas surging, and life being snuffed out in a catastrophic flood. However, this is not the final chapter; rather, it signifies a new beginning. From the wreckage, a balanced and harmonious world will arise, underscoring the cyclical notion intrinsic to Norse cosmology.

The residents of this captivating realm are thought to have originated from the first human pair, Ask and Embla, fashioned from trees by Odin and his brothers, Vili and Vé. This engaging narrative serves not only as an origin story but also emphasizes a crucial theme—the symbiotic relationship between humans and nature in this realm.

Asgard

Let us turn our attention to Asgard, the grand abode of the Aesir gods—who elicit both awe and reverence. This realm doesn't merely occupy any space; it sits on the topmost branch of Yggdrasil. Its fortress-like structure is unyielding and impregnable, designed with artistic mastery that encapsulates the essence of divine luxury. Picture golden rooftops shimmering in celestial light and intricately carved walls that stand as a testament to the elevated beings who reside here.

As we delve deeper, we come upon Valhalla, a monumental hall presided over by Odin himself. In this hall, warriors who have met their end in heroic combat are granted a second life and a place in this grand assembly. Adjacent to Valhalla is Vingolf, an elegant hall where goddesses and exceptional women convene. The very existence of these halls speaks volumes not only about valorous ideals but also about gender dynamics and the layers of social hierarchy deeply ingrained in the myths of the society that created them.

As for connectivity, let's not overlook that Asgard is part of a complex celestial architecture. In addition to the well-known Bifröst bridge, there are subtler, less obvious pathways connecting Asgard to realms like Alfheim, the luminous world of the Light Elves, and Vanaheim, the home of the Vanir gods. These intricate links symbolize the multi-layered relationships among these cosmic entities.

Even a realm as splendid as Asgard is not immune to the wheel of destiny. Its fate is irrevocably sealed in the prophecy of Ragnarök. Yet, herein lies the essence of its beauty—it is not merely a divine realm. It is a complex landscape pulsating with valor, poetry, ethical dilemmas, and a keen awareness of the cyclical nature of existence. What a fascinating mirror it offers, helping us understand the interplay between virtues and flaws, and between the ethereal and the mortal!

Vanaheim

Allow us to direct your imagination toward Vanaheim. You may not have heard of it as frequently as you have of Asgard or Midgard, but this realm plays a pivotal role in Norse cosmology. Unlike the warrior-like Aesir gods, the Vanir deities preside over an entirely different domain—fertility, prosperity, the earth, and all things natural. Picture vast landscapes flourishing in lush abundance: a symphony of greens and blues, a realm deeply intertwined with the elements.

The unique character of this realm extends to its architecture, which is as captivating as it is harmonious with nature. While exact details may be sparse, envision pastoral elegance—sprawling fields, meandering streams, and houses designed to harmonize with the contours of the land, incorporating living trees and stones into their structures. This place echoes the Vanir gods' intrinsic relationship with the natural world, offering a contrast to the celestial majesty of Asgard with an earthy grandeur that is entirely its own.

When it comes to rituals and practices, given the focus of the Vanir gods, imagine ceremonies replete with motifs of fertility and prosperity. This realm blurs the boundaries between the divine and the mundane. One could easily picture gods strolling through rich forests and abundant fields, playing an active role in the intricate cycles of life and death that govern the land.

You might wonder about Vanaheim's destiny in the cosmic prophecy of Ragnarök. Although its role may seem less defined than those of Asgard or Midgard, its significance should not be understated. Consider, for instance, Njord, who is said to return to Vanaheim during the cosmic dissolution. This seemingly minor detail in the grand narrative actually underscores Vanaheim's resilience and crucial role in the cycles of rebirth and renewal that govern the universe.

In this realm, we encounter divinity that is firmly rooted in the natural world. Vanaheim showcases an inherent sense of balance and interconnection, not only within its own scope but also in its complex relationships with other realms and their corresponding gods.

Jotunheim

Jotunheim is the dwelling place of the Jotnar, often translated as "giants." This realm presents a landscape as complex and nuanced as its inhabitants. While it may be tempting to envision it as a mere land of chaos and disarray, rest assured it is far more. It's a realm where raw power meets extreme conditions—not just icy mountains and vast wilderness, but also terrains that are exquisite displays of primal beauty: untamed, unforgiving, and infinitely fascinating.

Shall we discuss landmarks? Take, for instance, the fortress of Utgard, an awe-inspiring stronghold under the governance of the giant Utgard-Loki. This place challenges the very fabric of what we understand as reality. When Thor and Loki dare to step into this enigmatic castle, tasks that appear to be mundane take on complexities that shatter expectations, plunging them into an arena where the familiar morphs into the surreal.

The intelligence of the Jotnar should not be underestimated. They personify the realm they inhabit—a land that demands not just brawn but also a penetrating understanding of the laws governing nature. Here, survival is a craft, woven together by a blend of raw strength and finely honed strategy.

Although often considered separate from Asgard and Midgard, Jotunheim is anything but isolated. Mythic tales abound of gods and heroes journeying into this mysterious territory on quests that, while fraught with danger, are indispensable for cosmic equilibrium.

Regarding the realm's destiny in Ragnarök, the giants of Jotunheim are no mere bystanders. They will take sides, actively participating in seismic events aimed at unsettling the very foundations of the gods' realm. However, do not be quick to label them as mere agents of destruction. They are part and parcel of a cosmic cycle—a natural progression of decay and renewal that paves the way for a new world to rise from the ashes of the old.

So Jotunheim is a vital cog, a realm embodying the essence of natural law, chaos, intelligence, and cosmic balance. It is a realm that commands respect and evokes awe and wonder.

Niflheim

Let us journey to the realm of Niflheim, often referred to as the "Mist World", a domain defined less by what it contains than by what it lacks. Positioned at the roots of Yggdrasil, this world serves as a poetic canvas of absence, framed by ice, mist, and shadow. It is a place where the essence of existence itself seems to fray, a land governed by biting cold and perpetual darkness.

You might think Niflheim is an entirely desolate place, but there exists within it a segment governed by Hel, the goddess of death, that offers a fascinating counterpoint. Known as Helheim, this area within Niflheim presents a contrast to the realm's otherwise icy expanses.

We should also appreciate the elemental significance of Niflheim in the broader cosmogonic narrative. This realm existed even before gods and humans came into being, standing in polar opposition to Muspelheim, the world of fire. At the dawn of creation, the frigid environment of Niflheim met with the fierce heat of Muspelheim in the void known as Ginnungagap. From this union, Ymir was born, setting the stage for the birth of the nine realms. Isn't it fascinating that Niflheim, a realm seemingly devoid of life, plays an instrumental role in the genesis of existence?

Don't forget Hvergelmir, the "Roaring Kettle," a wellspring at the heart of Niflheim. This is no ordinary spring; it serves as the birthplace of all cold rivers and is vigilantly guarded by Nidhogg, the fearsome dragon that gnaws at Yggdrasil's roots. Here we find not just a geographical feature, but also a metaphysical focal point—a wellspring of energies as eternal as they are ever-changing.

For those who dare to venture into this perilous realm, Niflheim serves as a testing ground. Numerous myths narrate the stories of gods and heroes who brave its harsh elements, challenging not just their physical stamina but their spiritual resilience as well. While it may be a realm of trials, it is not without its hidden treasures, often concealed and requiring Herculean feats to uncover.

When it comes to the cataclysmic events of Ragnarök, Niflheim is not a passive observer. From this realm, the ship Naglfar sets sail, crafted from the nails of the dead, bearing legions that will clash with the gods. Yet even here, in the narrative of destruction, one finds traces of cyclical rebirth—indicating that even in absence or negation, Niflheim holds the keys to cosmic renewal.

Muspelheim

Let's turn our gaze toward the southernmost reaches of the Norse cosmos—Muspelheim. This realm defies simplistic interpretation. Known as the "Fire World," it serves as an elemental counterpart to Niflheim's frigid wastes. Imagine a land where molten lava flows like rivers, where infernos rise like mountains, and where the sky itself forms a tapestry of dancing embers. If Niflheim embodies the cosmos's inhale of cold, Muspelheim represents its exhale, warm and transformative, full of primordial vigor.

Guarding this incandescent world is Surtr, the fire giant whose name quite literally translates to "black" or "the swarthy one." Don't be too quick to label Muspelheim as merely a destructive realm; it is far from one-dimensional. It's not just about devastation; it's also about primal, creative energy.

Now let's examine how Muspelheim fits into the grand cosmic design. According to Norse tales of the beginning of time, Muspelheim is one of the two original realms, along with Niflheim. The heat from this land of fire met the ice from Niflheim, melting it and leading to the formation of life-giving droplets. Here, fire is a paradoxical force—it embodies both chaos and creation, underscoring its dualistic nature.

Though less frequented in tales of gods and heroes venturing into different worlds, the essence of Muspelheim—its fire—permeates Norse myths. It serves both as a deterrent and as a crucible for transformative challenges. When considering the symbolism of fire in these myths, we discover that it also represents passion, creativity, and deep insight—qualities as brilliant and unpredictable as the flames themselves.

Lastly, we shouldn't overlook Muspelheim's role in the apocalyptic events of Ragnarök. Surtr, brandishing his fiery blade, is prophesied to bring about the end of both gods and men by setting the world ablaze. Yet even in this cataclysmic act, Muspelheim contributes to a larger cosmic cycle. Destruction here is not an end; rather, it marks a new beginning and serves as a catalyst for universal rebirth.

Alfheim

Alfheim is a realm that stands apart in Norse cosmology like a rare gem in a jeweler's collection. Known as the "Elf World," Alfheim serves as the abode of the Light Elves. Although the elves may not be the protagonists of Norse myths—a role more often filled by the Aesir and Vanir gods—their realm offers an enchanting counterpoint among the nine worlds.

Freyr received Alfheim as a gift when he was but a child, illuminating the realm's strong links with fertility, sunlight, and prosperity—themes that resonate with the very essence of Freyr himself.

As for the realm's landscapes, imagine forests that sparkle as if kissed by dawn, meadows that shimmer like golden tapestries, and palaces crafted from crystal and gold. These aren't just fanciful descriptions; they suggest that Alfheim is also a metaphorical landscape, representing enlightenment, artistic inspiration, and eternal beauty. The air is infused with the aroma of blooming flowers, and the atmosphere pulsates with the celestial harmonies of elven music.

While myths may offer sparse details about Alfheim's role in cataclysmic events like Ragnarök, the realm's very existence serves a unique function. Consider it an antidote to the chaos and mortality present in other realms, a vivid illustration of existence in its most refined and elevated state. Amidst the interplay of various realms, Alfheim emerges as a constant reminder of the sublime heights that life can achieve.

Nidavellir/Svartalfheim

Nidavellir, also known as Svartalfheim, is a realm as fascinating as it is contrasting to the other worlds we have explored. Picture yourself descending into a labyrinthine universe, far beneath the surface, into the very roots of Yggdrasil. This is not a realm of verdant landscapes like Alfheim or radiant courts like Asgard. Instead, we find a subterranean marvel where the perpetual clang of hammers and anvils echoes through complex tunnels. Gems and minerals glow with intrinsic light, creating a mesmerizing tableau in eternal twilight.

Look closely, and you'll see that this underground realm serves, in many ways, as a mirror reflecting the characteristics of its inhabitants—the dwarves and the elusive black elves. The architecture here is breathtaking, comprising a combination of caves, tunnels, and grand halls resplendent with gleaming minerals and precious ores. It's a living palette of luminous gemstones and resplendent metals. The mastery of engineering is so advanced that this labyrinthine domain is nearly impregnable—even for gods.

The term "Svartalfheim," meaning "home of the black elves," adds an additional layer of mystery, suggesting a part of the realm that may house beings of a darker aspect. Their relationship to the dwarves remains shrouded in ambiguity, an enigmatic puzzle open to various interpretations. Are they the same beings, merely viewed through different cultural lenses, or is there a deeper, more complex relationship between them? The myths leave room for our imagination to wander.

Don't be deceived into thinking that because Nidavellir shies away from the cosmic spotlight, it is any less significant. Quite the contrary! This realm is the cradle where the very artifacts that define gods and heroes are crafted. It marries the material and the mystical, serving as a cornerstone of the Norse universe. Here, craftsmanship ascends to the level of sacred art. The dwarves, with their skill and shrewdness, educate even the gods about the hidden intricacies and splendors within the material world.

Thus, Nidavellir serves as the entire Norse cosmos's material anchor—a place where craft becomes an act of devotion and where the tactile and metaphysical merge in inseparable alchemy.

Helheim

We are about to delve into a realm shrouded in both awe and dread—Helheim, often simply called Hel. Now, if you're expecting a realm of eternal damnation akin to the Christian concept of Hell, prepare to be surprised. Helheim in Norse cosmology offers a more nuanced tapestry, far more complex than a mere dwelling of torment. It serves as the destination for souls who have not met their end in a heroic or remarkable manner in battle.

Governed by the elusive figure also named Hel, this realm resists easy interpretation. Imagine journeying deep beneath the roots of Yggdrasil to arrive at this mysterious world—a voyage filled with trials and tribulations. Upon entry, you'll encounter a towering wall and a massive gate. Ah, this is where Modgud stands—a sentinel who questions the motives and identities of those who dare to cross into this realm.

Within its boundaries, Helheim reveals its many facets. Various abodes accommodate the souls; some find places of relative comfort, enjoying eternal rest. Yet for others, particularly those considered dishonorable, grim quarters await. Hel's own hall, Eljudnir, serves as an expansive, somewhat dreary domain where she administers her judgments and ensures the proper functioning of this otherworldly realm.

Let's not overlook the landscape— as intricate and diverse as its inhabitants. Visualize fields of wilted flowers, dark, brooding forests, and rivers of obscure waterways. It's a tableau of melancholy rather than one of agony. Time in Helheim seems to stretch infinitely, allowing souls to ponder their past lives while the distant sounds of laughter and weeping merge into a haunting melody that can be considered life's ultimate chapter.

Then there's the river Gjoll, a significant feature that both demarcates Helheim and serves as a conduit. Crossing this river is a mandatory journey for the deceased, often aided by a maiden giantess. The bridge spanning the Gjoll, named Gjallarbrú, although covered in gold, offers far from a welcoming spectacle. It acts as a final checkpoint where souls are interrogated about their deeds and identities.

Among the realm's stories, none is more famous than that of Baldr, the beloved god of light and purity. Even this luminous deity found himself bound by the laws of Helheim after a conspiracy led by Loki resulted in his demise. Hermod, another son of Odin, led an ill-fated mission to retrieve Baldr, demonstrating that not even gods are exempt from the inexorable rules of this domain.

Helheim is not just an antithesis to the glory of Valhalla or Fólkvangr; it also defies the simplistic moral binaries often associated with afterlife realms in other mythologies. Here, we find neither heaven nor hell, but a multi-layered domain that explores various aspects of death. It stands as an everlasting testament to the inescapable reality of our mortality, yet it's also a realm far richer in symbolism and meaning than it is often credited for.

CHAPTER 5
The Norse Gods

Aesir Gods

The Aesir gods, also spelled "Æsir" in Old Norse, reside in the realm of Asgard. These deities held great importance among the Norse people and were held in high regard; this can be seen by their name "asa," used to refer to the gods in Norse mythology. When discussing these gods and goddesses, we touch upon nothing less than the very threads that weave the cosmos into a tapestry of life, power, and cosmic balance. Whether presiding over facets of war and wisdom or nuances of love and beauty, each deity serves essentially as a guardian of diverse aspects of existence itself.

However, let's avoid the trap of reducing them to mere categories or lists. To truly grasp the essence of these gods, we must delve into the intricate labyrinth of their personal relationships—examining alliances formed and betrayed, as well as bonds both familial and otherwise. Far from being static figures immortalized in ancient stories, these deities are dynamic entities, continuously evolving.

In the interplay among these deities and the delicate equilibrium they collectively maintain, we begin to comprehend their true nature. Understanding one deity illuminates aspects of another; they are inherently interdependent, each relying on the other to sustain the cosmic harmony governing all things. It is within this context that the narrative truly gains complexity and intrigue.

These interactions, alliances, and occasional betrayals provide the most genuine portrayals of these gods and goddesses. Capable of growth, subject to failure, and endowed with complexities, they serve not just as divine rulers but also as mirrors reflecting the intricacies of existence itself.

Odin

Odin, the Allfather, is a divine paradox, a god who embodies a myriad of contrasting qualities—from wisdom and war to the subtleties of poetry and even deception. Through him, one gains a better understanding of how the Norse people grappled with the intricate layers of existence itself.

The insatiable thirst for knowledge defines Odin. His quest for wisdom is so intense that it led him to give up an eye at Mimir's Well. Ah, the poetic elegance of the sacrifice—giving up a part of oneself to gain a fuller understanding of the world! Add to this his two trusted ravens, Huginn and Muninn, embodiments of thought and memory, who traverse the realms daily to bring back whispers of information. This quest for wisdom makes Odin not merely wise, but the quintessential seeker within Norse mythology. But the nuances don't end there. Odin is also hailed as a god of war and strategic brilliance. One doesn't simply pray to Odin for brute strength; one invokes him when seeking the intelligence to win battles. The symbol of his martial prowess is his spear, Gungnir, a weapon so precise it never misses its target. This points to Odin's calculated approach to conflict, an intricate dance between might and mind.

Let's not forget his poetic sensibilities. Odin, you see, is credited with acquiring the mead of poetry. The soft mellowness of this mead serves as a symbol for artistic expression, a tender counterpoint to his warlike tendencies. Here, we see a rounded, emotionally textured portrait of masculinity—strength harmonized with sensitivity and wisdom.

The complexity of Odin is further highlighted by his darker traits. This god has a knack for cunning and deceit. He wears disguises; he employs subterfuge. One is left to ponder whether this trickery is a necessary tool, born out of his colossal responsibility for the cosmos, or whether it casts a shadow, revealing a more selfish layer in his endless pursuit for knowledge and control.

The web of relationships that Odin weaves is equally revealing. His partnership with Frigga, his wife, bestows upon them both the gift of prophecy. Yet it is only Frigga who knows the full scope of what the future holds. Odin is also a father to gods like Thor and Baldr, each a reflection of a facet of Odin's own intricate nature—whether it be valor and might or purity and beauty.

Then there's the tragic beauty of Odin's fate, the apocalypse known as Ragnarök. Odin knows it will bring his end. Yet, undeterred, he continues to gather fallen warriors in Valhalla, preparing them for the ultimate confrontation. Here, his sense of duty and stoicism reveals yet another facet of his multifaceted personality. Odin serves as a cosmic prism, refracting the numerous complexities of life and governance. He invites us to explore these aspects within ourselves and the universe at large. Through him, the Norse confronted dichotomies—power and vulnerability, wisdom and ignorance—adding a valuable dimension to our eternal quest for understanding.

Frigga

Frigga, often eclipsed by the flamboyance of her husband, Odin, is a goddess of her own substance and domain. One might easily assume that as the Queen of Asgard, she merely exists in Odin's shadow. Such an assumption is far from accurate and does little justice to her rich, multi-layered persona.

Frigga is not merely a goddess of home and hearth; she is also a deity of wisdom, intuition, and incredible resilience. Much like her husband, Frigga possesses knowledge of the future but chooses to keep it veiled in secrecy. Consider this stoicism; it adds another layer to her personality, a quiet form of strength that knows how to hold its tongue and bear the weight of destiny. It is as if she holds the world's secrets within her, creating a subtle contrast to Odin's constant attempts to manipulate fate. Now, step with me into the domestic sphere she governs—marriage, family, domestic life. Aren't these the very bricks that construct the edifice of a society? In her quiet way, she is the guardian of community values, the one invoked during childbirth to ensure a safe passage into life. Far from being trivial, these domains are the pillars of civilization, the invisible threads that tie a community together.

But her wisdom and cunning are not confined to her domain. Recall the tale of her son, Baldr, destined by prophecy to die. Unable to rewrite fate, Frigga employs her ingenuity to extract promises from every element on Earth not to harm her child. True, she ultimately fails—Baldr dies from a mistletoe arrow—but consider the lengths she goes to and the intricacies of her attempt to outwit destiny. Here, we get a glimpse of her skill, her art of maneuvering deities and elements to achieve her objectives. And don't be misled. While the Norse sagas rarely cast her as a warrior, that should not be mistaken for passivity. No, her power manifests in a more subtle form—navigating the social and domestic spheres where, believe it or not, the stakes are often highest. Birth, marriage, death—aren't these the crux of human experience?

Let your gaze fall upon the spindle and distaff often associated with her. At first glance, these may seem like mere tokens of domestic labor, but they are so much more. In the spinning and weaving of these tools, she shapes destiny itself, pulling together the threads of the past, present, and future into a coherent tapestry. Here she sits, not just as a homemaker but as a shaper of destiny. Frigga invites us to see that there is power in the domestic, wisdom in subtlety, and that the pillars of society often stand in spaces considered "conventional." In her, we discover that the seemingly mundane can be deeply profound and that life's quieter aspects can hold a beauty and significance all their own.

Thor

Thor, the Thunder God, is a figure who seems to transcend time and culture. With his mane of red hair, a voice that resonates like thunder itself, and a hammer that has become synonymous with both destruction and protection, Thor is a deity who mirrors the raw energy we find in nature and indeed within ourselves. Defender of not just Asgard but also Midgard—the realm of humans—his hammer, Mjölnir, is more than just a chunk of metal; it is a divine tool with enchanting properties, created by the skillful hands of dwarves. When Thor throws it, the hammer returns to him, as if magnetically linked to its master. The very image of this hammer was often worn as an amulet, something that people held close to their hearts for protection. Here, the hammer serves dual roles, embodying both the potential for cataclysmic destruction and the comforting assurance of safeguarding. Thor, the epitome of martial skill, possesses a depth that extends beyond the battlefield. Unlike Odin, who envelops himself in a cloud of wisdom and complexity, or Loki, the trickster par excellence, Thor's complexity is rooted in his emotional richness. He is not an unreadable god; his feelings are laid bare for all to see. When he is angry, it often stems from a deep sense of justice and a desire to shield those he is bound to protect. His emotions make him both mighty and vulnerable, pulling him into precarious situations while also rendering him endearing and relatable to us mere mortals.

Unlike Odin, Thor is incredibly approachable. His divine duty often entails protecting humanity from celestial threats, such as giants who disrupt cosmic equilibrium. He is the god next door, so to speak—an approachable figure, the sort of deity with whom you feel you could share a feast, amidst roaring laughter and jovial banter.

Let's add another layer to Thor's persona: humor. Yes, you read that correctly. Whether disguising himself as a bride to outwit a giant and reclaim his stolen hammer or engaging in contests that reveal his charming overconfidence, Thor is not devoid of comedic elements. These moments of levity do not undermine his seriousness but enrich his character, painting a portrait of a god who knows not just battle but also the joys of life. Look closer, and you will see the nuances in his family ties. A devoted husband to Sif and a complex but loving father to his children, Thor instills values of valor and integrity. Then there's Loki, his trickster brother, who may irk him to no end but also holds a special place in his life. Their relationship encompasses contrasting emotions—irritation, respect, rivalry—yet one gets the feeling that they complete each other in a most peculiar way. But, let's not forget the legacy that reverberates through our own world: Thursday, or "Thor's Day," stands as a lasting testament to the virtues he embodies. It serves as a weekly reminder that the qualities that define Thor—strength, courage, and a protective nature—are not just distant, godly traits but virtues that can guide us in our everyday lives.

Sif

Sif is a goddess whose presence is often overshadowed by her larger-than-life husband, Thor. However, she is far from a mere supporting character in the grand play of gods and goddesses. She embodies facets of femininity, fertility, and stability that not only anchor Thor but also ripple through the cosmic design of the Norse world. Her famed golden hair is not simply a beauty statement.

Consider it instead as an extended metaphor: her locks are like fields of wheat, shimmering in the sun. She stands as a symbol of the earth's fertility, embodying the very elements of growth and renewal that sustain both gods and humans. When you look at Sif, you are not merely gazing at Thor's wife; you are encountering the life-giving essence that feeds the world. Of course, you may know her story through Loki's mischievous act of cutting off her golden locks. But pause here: this is not just a casual prank. It's an act that disrupts the very balance of the divine and natural worlds, given the symbolic weight her hair carries. This incident becomes the catalyst for a grand adventure, leading to the dwarves crafting not only a new set of golden hair for her but also other magical objects, including Thor's famed hammer, Mjölnir. She is not just a bystander in this tale but a focal point that sets significant events into motion.

Let's not forget her graceful resilience; she welcomes her new hair, which grows back endowed with its original, life-giving essence. The dynamics between Sif and Thor are illuminating. While Thor is often absorbed in his battles against giants and cosmic threats, Sif remains the grounding force, the emotional hearth that brings balance. She represents the quiet stability that complements Thor's more tempestuous and externalized form of heroism. In Sif, we witness a different kind of heroism, one that may not brandish weapons in the open field but maintains the world's equilibrium in a subtler, yet equally vital, manner.

While textual references to Sif may be scant, what we do know of her points to a quieter form of strength. She doesn't engage in intrigues or seek to stand at the center of cosmic dramas. Instead, she seems focused on her domain: the earth, the hearth, the home. Her heroism isn't flaunted, but that doesn't make it any less important.

Here's what we must understand: the subtlety in her presence should not be confused with insignificance. Sif embodies virtues that may not grab headlines—patience, nurturing, wisdom—but they are fundamental in maintaining the balance of the world. While she may not wield a hammer or fight giants, her actions and qualities are the very threads that keep the fabric of the world from unraveling.

Tyr

Tyr is a god whose name may not resonate as loudly today as those of Odin or Thor, but he is nevertheless an entity rich in meaning. What intrigues us about Tyr is not only his association with warfare but also the form of combat he embodies—just, lawful, and governed by principles essential for any society aspiring to be more than a mere horde of chaotic elements.

The tale of the binding of Fenrir, the fearsome wolf, showcases Tyr's essence. He places his hand in the wolf's mouth as a guarantee while the gods bind the creature. When the wolf realizes it has been tricked, Tyr loses his hand. Yet, don't see this merely as a loss; regard it as an emblematic sacrifice for the greater good. Tyr's missing hand serves as a perpetual reminder of the personal sacrifices required to uphold justice and maintain the balance of the cosmos. His story is not just about physical loss; it's a metaphorical narrative that underscores what it takes to uphold a stable world order. Tyr's role doesn't stop at courageous acts. He is deeply involved in the machinery of governance. Tyr is the god you invoke in matters of law, in judgments, and in decisions. Have you heard of the Thing, the Norse assembly for legal matters? Tyr's association with this institution demonstrates his position as a god of community and collective justice. His is not a form of vindictive or arbitrary justice but one focused on preserving harmony within society.

His spirit embodies martial vigor. Imagine him with a sword, if you will. However, his is not the combat of brute force, like Thor's; it is warfare marked by discipline, strategy, and a set of ethical rules. Tyr embodies the honorable warrior, one who respects his opponent and fights not just for the sake of fighting, but with a higher purpose and set of rules in mind.

The rune associated with Tyr, known as Tiwaz, takes the form of an arrow pointing upward. This is more than mere symbolism; the rune represents justice, sacrifice, and rationality. It serves as a reminder that, for society to function, decisions must be made with careful, rational aim—much like how an arrow shot must be aimed true. The rune points upward, symbolizing a reach for higher ideals and mirroring Tyr's concerns with moral and societal equilibrium. In a broader historical context, you might be interested to learn that Tyr was once possibly a chief god, somewhat akin to Odin's later role. Although his status shifted as Odin gained prominence, Tyr's sphere of influence, focused on ethical and judicial matters, remained constant. This historical evolution reflects the changing values and needs of society, but it doesn't diminish the intrinsic qualities that Tyr represents.

Loki

Loki refuses to be confined by any neat categories that we often use to define gods or even human characters. Is he good or evil? The answer isn't straightforward. He is a shape-shifter in every sense, oscillating between the roles of trickster, villain, helper, and occasionally, even hero.

The more we explore Loki's multifaceted nature, the more we realize he embodies qualities so rich that they almost defy description. Loki is a deity of mischief and unpredictability. But here's the interesting part: labeling him simply as a chaotic element would do him an injustice. Loki revels in creating turmoil, it's true, but not all his actions lead to destruction. Remember how Thor received his hammer, Mjölnir? That was Loki's doing. In many such tales, Loki starts a fire only to put it out, savoring the ensuing drama and often benefiting from it. So his chaos isn't mindless; it's a labyrinth of intricate plans that require a deep understanding of situations and personalities. While Odin seeks wisdom to understand fate and Thor uses his raw power to confront challenges, Loki employs cunning to weave through the threads of destiny.

A deity who defies not only moral categories but also the very boundaries of form and identity: that's Loki for you. He shape-shifts not just in bodily form—transforming into a mare, a salmon, or even a mosquito—but also in the psychological realm. This fluidity allows him to challenge norms and perceptions, forcing gods and mortals alike to reconsider established hierarchies. Don't forget that Loki is a Jotunn, a giant, yet lives among the gods as one of them. What a perfect symbol of an eternal outsider!

Loki's complex personality is even mirrored in his offspring. As the father of Hel, Jormungandr, and Fenrir, he contributes to the darker aspects of the cosmos. But, don't forget that he is also the mother—yes, you heard it right—of Odin's horse, Sleipnir, thereby adding constructive elements to the world as well. It's as if Loki's familial roles themselves are displaying both hues of creation and destruction. Consider Loki's grand, almost theatrical role in the apocalyptic events of Ragnarök. He leads the forces against the gods with whom he once frolicked. Yet even in this act, his characteristic ambiguity prevails. The world that he helps to end makes way for a new, reborn universe. In this, Loki becomes an agent of change, a manifestation of entropy that, paradoxically, leads to renewal.

Baldr

Baldr, a deity so unlike the others, shines brilliantly amidst a cast of complex and often morally ambiguous gods. You see, Baldr is a beacon of purity, innocence, and light. His very name signifies bravery, but not the sort displayed on battlefields by Thor or Tyr. Rather, his is the bravery of being vulnerable, of being pure in a world filled with complexities. A god so radiant, fair-skinned, and handsome that he literally lights up every space he occupies, Baldr's allure is more than mere aesthetic beauty; it's a window into his soul. He represents wisdom, kindness, and grace in such measure that he is universally beloved—by gods and all other beings. His residence, a place called Breidablik, is so pure that nothing unclean can even exist there. You can imagine this realm as a sanctuary where the essence of goodness and purity is perfectly crystallized.

Let's delve into a tale that casts a shadow over this luminescent figure: Baldr's haunting dreams of his own demise. Despite the oaths extracted by his mother, Frigga, from all elements and beings to not harm him, it was a tiny mistletoe that became his undoing. Frigga considered it too insignificant to swear an oath. But Loki, ever the mischief-maker, used this oversight to bring about Baldr's death. The impact reverberated far beyond personal tragedy; it tore asunder the cosmic equilibrium and set the stage for Ragnarök, the end of the world. What is deeply touching is that after Baldr's death, the universe itself weeps. Plants, animals, gods, and all beings mourn his passing. His loss is felt not just as a familial or communal tragedy but as a cosmic imbalance. Through Baldr, we confront the vulnerability of goodness itself. Even among gods of immense power and warriors of great valor, the quality of pure goodness isn't invincible, yet its absence leaves a void that the whole world feels.

Think not that Baldr's tale is just a mournful saga consigned to the annals of mythology. Prophecies speak of a time post-Ragnarök when he will return, rising like the sun to illuminate a reborn world and ruling it alongside his resurrected brother, Hodr. Baldr serves as a glimmering thread of hope and renewal. So, while gods like Odin and Thor grapple with cosmic decay and the inexorable march toward chaos, Baldr stands as a reminder of the virtues to which we must cling: purity, light, and goodness. His life and prophesized return speak to the fragile yet undying power of these virtues in a universe too often shrouded in darkness and complexity.

Nanna

A figure who often stays in the background, somewhat eclipsed by her illustrious husband, Nanna is a Norse goddess who provides us with a fascinating lens through which to view crucial elements like devotion, love, and the cycle of life and death that are so intricately woven into the human experience.

Nanna is the quintessence of grace and fidelity. Beside Baldr, she is not just a loving spouse but also a living representation of profound commitment. It's absolutely captivating to note that amid a celestial ensemble rife with complicated entanglements and betrayals, the relationship between Nanna and Baldr offers a refreshing simplicity—a love that is unconditional and harmonious. The couple's bond echoes the purity and light embodied by Baldr himself.

It is Baldr's tragedy that not only redefines Nanna's character but also adds an indelible hue to the overall narrative. Upon hearing the devastating news of Baldr's demise, Nanna's heart breaks. She passes away and is reunited with her husband in the afterlife as they both are burned on the same funeral pyre. Imagine the intensity of such love—a devotion so overpowering that it transcends the veil between life and death, escorting her to Helheim, where she joins Baldr in the realm of the departed.

Would you believe that even from beyond, Nanna continues to participate in the lives of her loved ones? From the dark corners of the underworld, she sends back gifts: a robe for Frigga and a ring for Fulla. These are not mere objects;

they are heartwarming symbols of her everlasting compassion and warmth. Nanna's post-mortem tokens remind us that even in her absence, her nurturing spirit remains intact, reinforcing her identity and the love she carries for those she left behind.

While Nanna may not be as conspicuous as Odin with his wisdom or Loki with his trickery, her story accentuates a different but equally important aspect—the profound nature of familial and spousal bonds. In a world often characterized by gods and goddesses involved in tempestuous relationships fraught with conflict and deceit, Nanna serves as a cornerstone of a love that is both ardent and stable.

As we project into the future—into a world reborn after Ragnarök where Baldr is prophesized to return and rule—consider the weight of Nanna's choice to accompany him in death. Her presence in the afterlife implicitly anticipates her own resurrection in a dance of undying love that not even the apocalypse could halt.

Heimdall

Heimdall stands as a guardian figure at the twilight zone between the divine and mortal spheres. Often referred to as the "Watchman of the Gods," Heimdall provides a fascinating counterpoint to the tumultuous energies that populate the Norse universe.

Equipped with senses so extraordinarily refined that he can hear the grass growing and see hundreds of miles even in the dead of night, it's almost as if he was designed for his role: the eternal guardian of Bifrost, the dazzling rainbow bridge linking the mortal world of Midgard to the divine realm of Asgard. But let's not mistake his vigilance for mere watchfulness—it represents a proactive stance, that of a sentinel prepared to sound the Gjallarhorn to signal the coming of Ragnarök.

His origins are veiled in a kind of poetic mystery. Born of nine mothers, who were sisters and perhaps even representations of the sea, he is the god of liminality, existing on multiple borders simultaneously, both literally and symbolically.

Heimdall is not just a cosmic guardian; he also delves into the heart of human concerns. During his sojourn into Midgard under the guise of Rig, he fathers the classes of humanity—thralls, peasants, and nobles—thus shaping the social structure much as he shapes the borders between realms. He is not just a boundary keeper but also a creator of societal order.

Adding a dash of drama is Heimdall's rivalry with Loki. Both possess the ability to shape-shift, both have mysterious origins, and both wield unique skills. Yet, where Loki employs his talents to create disarray, Heimdall uses his to foster order. It's like watching two sides of the same coin in eternal opposition. Their ultimate duel, destined to occur during Ragnarök, symbolizes the cosmic tension between order and chaos.

The moment Heimdall sounds the Gjallarhorn during Ragnarök captures the essence of his character brilliantly. While that horn blast signifies the world's end, it also serves as a rallying cry, a call to arms for the gods to engage in the ultimate battle. In that singular act, Heimdall embodies his core traits—vigilance, transition, and cyclical renewal.

Bragi

Bragi, the Norse god of poetry, eloquence, and music, introduces a soothing melody into a pantheon more accustomed to the cacophonies of war and trickery. The very etymology of "Bragi" likely derives from the Old Norse verb "braga," which means "to celebrate" or "to poetize." It is precisely through these lenses that we explore his intriguing features.

Commonly portrayed with a long, flowing beard, Bragi has a unique detail: runes etched onto his tongue. These are not mere decorations; they are symbols of arcane knowledge, emphasizing Bragi's mastery over the spoken and sung word. His eloquence transcends mere artistic expression; it verges on the magical, echoing the Norse tradition of "galdr," where the utterance of certain phrases can invoke magical phenomena. In his domain, words have the potency to shape reality.

Bragi is married to Idun, the goddess who guards the apples of eternal youth. This is not just a random marital alliance among gods. Consider the symbolism: Idun embodies rejuvenation, while Bragi personifies the medium that preserves history and heroism. Together, they represent an elegant cycle of renewal and remembrance. Through their union, the gods are offered a nuanced form of immortality—rejuvenation for the body through Idun and for the legacy through Bragi's poetic prowess.

Where does one usually encounter Bragi? Not on the battlefield, but in grand halls, where his poetic compositions serve dual functions: as entertainment and as historical chronicles. Picture him welcoming deceased heroes to Valhalla, transforming their life stories into poetic legacies, thereby immortalizing their valor. He essentially serves as the grandmaster of ceremonies for the afterlife, ensuring that heroes are eternally celebrated.

As for his earthly impact, the skalds—the wandering poets of Norse society—hold Bragi in a special place of reverence. These skalds do more than just narrate tales; they weave the fabric of history and culture. By inspiring the skalds, Bragi plays an indispensable role in the transference of knowledge and the preservation of cultural heritage.

To add a layer of historical enigma, there are suggestions that Bragi might originally have been a 9th-century court poet named Bragi Boddason. Is the god an elevated version of the historical poet, or did the poet model himself after the pre-existing god? The answer remains elusive, but this uncertainty adds a delightful layer of complexity to Bragi's already multifaceted existence.

Forseti

Forseti—a beacon of calm in a cosmos frequently marred by strife and conflict—is the god of justice, law, and reconciliation. This role, exceedingly specialized, is utterly essential for preserving order among gods and mortals alike. The son of Baldr and Nanna, Forseti naturally inherits an intuitive sense of fairness and an unyielding commitment to resolving disputes.

Shall we take a tour of his divine residence? Known as Glitnir, this celestial hall shimmers in silver and is upheld by pillars of pure gold. Far from being merely a divine dwelling, Glitnir functions as the ultimate court of arbitration. Anyone entering this luminous space in search of judgment finds more than just a sympathetic ear; they encounter an impeccable resolution. The architecture itself seems to anticipate the essence of true justice—pure, enriching, and eminently fair. Here, one can feel the palpable intensity of Forseti's virtues.

Consider the aura of this god. Intellectually astute and linguistically refined, Forseti employs his faculties to serve as the ultimate mediator. He does not operate on a whim but on considered balance, listening attentively to both sides before issuing a verdict. What defines his decisions is impartiality and the meticulous application of laws, both celestial and terrestrial.

Forseti is not enamored with the valor of warriors or the grandiosity of heroic quests. Rather, his preoccupation is the very framework of society—the rules and codes governing interactions. Particularly within the ambiguous corridors of law, where right and wrong blur, Forseti's expertise shines. Historical runic inscriptions and ancient sagas suggest that human leaders often invoked his wisdom when instituting new laws or delivering judgments.

Take, for instance, a story in which tensions between two factions teeter dangerously close to violent eruption. It is Forseti who steps in, offering an ingeniously fair solution that both sides accept. His intervention not only defuses an immediate crisis but also serves as a legal precedent for future conflicts. Thus, Forseti is not a static deity but an adaptive one, capable of evolving while adhering to the foundational principles of law.

Let's also consider the symbolic tools associated with him—an axe that diverges from the conventional connotations of warfare. Instead, this axe appears as an object used in legal rituals, symbolizing that disputes should be severed by judgment rather than by violence. Featured extensively in various texts, this tool encapsulates Forseti's devotion to mediation and the law as vehicles for social cohesion. The influence Forseti wields is significant. Especially in a society where disagreements over territory, resources, and honor are commonplace, the need for a god like Forseti is deeply and intensely felt.

Hermóðr

Hermóðr, often considered a son of Odin, serves as the gods' brave and unfailingly loyal messenger. One of his most legendary acts—his sojourn into the underworld to negotiate the release of his deceased brother, Baldr—serves as an extraordinary focal point. This journey allows us not only to delve into the intricate relationships among the Aesir family but also to explore deeper, more existential Norse concepts such as bravery, loyalty, and the mysteries of the afterlife. Baldr is dead, and the celestial realms are drenched in sorrow. Drawing upon courage and loyalty that few possess, Hermóðr steps forward to volunteer for a treacherous mission: to journey to Helheim and plead for his brother's return. He mounts Sleipnir, Odin's steed, and steers through landscapes as perilous as they are uncharted. This is no ordinary mission. The daunting quest reveals the very essence of Hermóðr's character. Although not a warrior god in the traditional sense, his bravery takes a different form—one that involves venturing into the unknown, guided solely by his loyalty to his family. His father, Odin, and his brother, Baldr—these relationships anchor his existence. He meets every hurdle on his journey with stubborn resilience that propels him forward until he finally stands before Hel to negotiate for Baldr's release. Consider the art of diplomacy. Standing before Hel in her own realm, Hermóðr demonstrates extraordinary negotiating skills. Hel agrees to release Baldr, but only if every living and non-living entity will weep for him, thereby affirming his universal belovedness. Although the mission ultimately fails—a lone being refuses to weep, thanks to Loki's perpetual schemes—Hermóðr's valor and diplomacy do not go unacknowledged. Upon his return, even bearing disappointing news, the gods eagerly await him to commend his bravery and resourcefulness.

What about Hermóðr's emotional fabric? It's seldom discussed but is an integral aspect of his character. Can you feel the weight of his mission, replete with personal loss and cosmic implications? Despite these burdens, Hermóðr proceeds, fueled by profound love for his family and a robust sense of duty. This emotional fortitude imbues his persona with remarkable depth, distinguishing him from other, perhaps more straightforward deities in Norse mythology. Don't overlook the cosmological undertones of Hermóðr's tale. His journey across the Bifrost, through Midgard, and into the very bowels of Helheim illuminates the Norse vision of a multi-tiered universe. Moreover, his dealings with Hel touch upon the complex questions of destiny and universal laws, principles so unyielding that even divine interventions find them difficult to bend.

Dellingr

Dellingr—the God of Dawn. At first glance, one might think that Dellingr has a lesser role, but the more we delve into his essence, the more we realize his importance. Through Dellingr, we gain insight into the Nordic understanding of time, transitions, and the very cycle of life itself.

Consider Dellingr as part of an extraordinary family. He is the third spouse of Nótt, the very embodiment of night. Together, they have a child, Dagr, who personifies day. What a magical household this is! It's a home where opposites not only attract but also complement one another beautifully. Nótt, shrouded in the peaceful mysteries of the night, and Dellingr, the herald of the first light that scatters the shadows, come together to produce Dagr—the full, glorious light of day.

Make no mistake: Dellingr is not a passive bystander in this cosmic dance of light and darkness. He is an active participant in the miraculous transition from night to day. Imagine the Scandinavians, living through long and severe winters, when the cloak of darkness seems almost eternal. For them, the dawn—personified by Dellingr—becomes a moment of pure magic, tinged with hope and the promise of a new day.

Let's examine his physical characteristics, which are albeit sparsely detailed. Most accounts depict him as radiating a comforting, warm light, reminiscent of dawn itself. Unlike many gods who are war-ready, Dellingr's power lies not in weaponry or battle prowess but in that first light—a beacon that guides people, allowing them to see and navigate the world afresh every morning.

His persona, too, would naturally be of a gentler nature. He symbolizes the hope and optimism that are inextricably linked with the dawn, contrasting sharply with gods known for their valor in battle. Dellingr, in essence, represents that tranquil moment, that deep inhalation before a day filled with countless possibilities unfolds.

Let's examine Dellingr from a cosmological viewpoint. His cyclic relationship with Nótt and their offspring, Dagr, encapsulates the Norse understanding of time as an eternal wheel, forever spinning and renewing. This idea is not isolated; it echoes throughout Norse cosmology, most notably in the cataclysmic concept of Ragnarök.

Hoenir

Hoenir—a god who might initially appear as a supporting actor in the grand Norse theatrical play but who, upon closer inspection, holds significant roles. Hoenir is somewhat like an enigmatic character in a complex novel, a figure who quietly holds the strings to fundamental questions about Norse culture, resilience, and diplomacy.

Isn't it fascinating that Hoenir is one of the few gods to survive the cataclysmic events of Ragnarök? This single detail speaks volumes about his resilience and role in the cosmic order. It's as if he has been chosen to bear witness to both the end and a fresh beginning, granting him a place in the eternal cycle of destruction and renewal.

Nicknamed "the Long-legged" or "the Swift," Hoenir is described as possessing noteworthy agility and speed. Imagine him as someone who is swift not only of foot but also of mind. It's easy to see how these traits mirror essential human capabilities, particularly the abilities to adapt and navigate—skills crucial for survival in the rugged terrains of ancient Scandinavia.

Let's discuss the Aesir-Vanir war, a cosmic conflict that ended in a truce. At the conclusion of hostilities, hostages were exchanged as tokens of peace. Among these, Hoenir was sent to the Vanir, a gesture symbolizing trust and diplomatic intent. While among the Vanir, it is said that Hoenir often hesitated and leaned on the counsel of his companion, Mimir. This peculiar behavior has led to varied interpretations. Some consider him indecisive or even ineffective; others see him as contemplative and reflective. However, consider this: being chosen as a peace emissary is no small feat. It reveals high regard for his diplomatic qualities. The challenges he faces among the Vanir may tell us more about the intricacies of intercultural interactions and diplomacy than about Hoenir's own capabilities.

The apex of his resilience comes into focus with Ragnarök. Emerging from this universal cataclysm, Hoenir is fated to play a role in the reconstruction of a new world. This continuity, from involvement in the creation of humanity to surviving Ragnarök, encapsulates him as a figure of both beginnings and eternal returns. It adds a poetic touch, lending depth to a character otherwise considered secondary.

Hodr

Hodr—sometimes spelled Hodur or Höðr—offers a compelling narrative tinged with irony and tragedy. At first glance, Hodr is easily defined by his one cataclysmic act: the accidental killing of his brother Baldr. Yet, upon closer examination, Hodr's life and actions provide a rich tableau for pondering age-old questions of fate, agency, and vulnerability.

First, let's examine the most distinctive aspect of Hodr: his blindness. Unlike gods who exude physical strength or combat expertise, Hodr stands apart, not for what he can do, but for what he cannot. His blindness transcends mere physicality to become a metaphor. It crystallizes existential themes such as destiny and free will, serving as an allegory for the limitations faced by each one of us, god or human. It's as if Hodr, unable to see the outcome of his actions or the horizon of his destiny, epitomizes the human condition in its rawest form.

The event that defines Hodr's life—the killing of Baldr—is far from a simple affair. Deceived by the cunning Loki, Hodr fires the mistletoe arrow that seals his brother's fate. What is crucial to understand is Hodr's innocence; his act contains no malevolence, only a tragic misunderstanding manipulated by external forces. Here, Hodr's vulnerability comes to the fore, revealing the soft underbelly of his character. He is a god dependent on the interpretations and guidance of others, leaving him susceptible to exploitation and deception.

His story confronts us with the grim aspects of existence: the inherent limitations we all possess and how those limitations can lead to profound tragedies. Hodr serves almost as a mirror reflecting the complexity of life itself, personifying the human predicament but with the stakes amplified by divinity.

Don't overlook the glimmer of redemption that shades Hodr's destiny. After his death, he finds himself in Helheim, united with Baldr. This reunion, clouded by the past yet suffused with the inevitability of destiny, embodies themes of forgiveness and familial love. It's as though the universe, or the forces that dictate Norse mythology, grants Hodr a second chance at reconciliation—a small comfort, perhaps, but one that allows his narrative to harbor a flicker of hope, even in the realm of the dead.

Lodurr

Lodurr, a deity whose very name seems to play hide-and-seek in the labyrinth of language, comes to life as we open an ancient tome, seeking whispers and hints about a figure who largely opts to remain in the shadows of Norse mythology. The moment we touch upon Lodurr, we are engaging with the very pulse of vital force—the elemental surge that fuels life, action, and the resilience to defy overwhelming odds.

Now consider this tantalizing possibility: Could Lodurr be Loki under another name? The idea isn't as implausible as it might initially appear. Linguistic parallels between "Lodurr" and "Loki" have ignited scholarly debate, and they share thematic strands as well. Both are tied to transformation and an intrinsic, vital force. This interconnection gives rise to an interpretation of Lodurr as a god not only of creative energies but also of chaos—a dual nature at its finest. Picture a force that serves as both the architect of change and the unpredictable maelstrom that upends the order of life and death.

But what do we know of Lodurr's personality, or how the ancient Norse venerated him? Here, we enter a misty terrain where facts are scarce. However, the absence of information should not lead us to underestimate his importance. Lodurr is credited with bestowing upon humanity the gift of life force itself—a foundational gift that perhaps echoes traits of resilience and even passion. Imagine a force so intrinsic that it courses through the veins of every living being, urging them to live, to strive, to survive. Such is the realm of Lodurr: enigmatic, yet undeniably integral.

Mani

Let us now set our sights skyward, into the mesmerizing darkness of the Norse night sky. Can you see it? There—gliding effortlessly in a celestial chariot—is Mani, the god personifying the Moon. While the Sun is magnificent in its constant blaze, in contrast the Moon, a celestial body, offers us only subtle, fluctuating glimmers of light. Mani, much like the moon he represents, is a deity of subtleties, intricacies, and fascinating dichotomies.

Imagine Mani riding his chariot through the night, perpetually chased by a wolf named Hati. What a vivid spectacle, one that represents not just a nightly chase but also the framework for the phases of the moon. Mani isn't merely a god who appears and fades; he is a god of cycles, of transitions from new to full, of change, and of the inevitable renewals that mark both cosmic and earthly realms. He embodies the passage of time, the changing seasons, and even the great circle of life and death.

Let's delve into a quirk in Mani's lore: a quality that could be seen as both unsettling and intriguing. He is described as kidnapping children and a man named Bil to become his celestial companions. At first glance, the notion of abduction sends shivers down the spine. But there's another layer here. Could this act not also be an offering of sanctuary, a divine "world apart" from earthly sorrows or mundane realities? Therein lies the duality of Mani, a god who both shapes time and provides an escape from it.

Often, Mani's character leads us toward the quieter corners of Norse spirituality. Unlike the Sun, which offers a bright, unforgiving light, the Moon and Mani offer a softer illumination. Theirs is a realm of shadows, of subdued light, of quietude and introspection. Think of Mani as the patron of inner worlds, inviting us to delve into our deepest consciousness and reflect on the hidden layers of existence not immediately visible to the naked eye.

Mani's cosmic dance with danger—the ceaseless pursuit by the wolf Hati—infuses Mani's tale with a certain tension between order and chaos, a foundational theme in Norse cosmology. Mani navigates the celestial sphere, always a hair's breadth away from his predator. No, Mani is not a warrior god; he wields no thunderous hammer. Yet, in his delicate evasion, he embodies a different form of heroism: a quiet strength rooted in persistence and the maintenance of cosmic and natural cycles.

Meili

Let us delve into one of the lesser-known figures in Norse mythology: a god named Meili who shares the celestial stage with his mighty brother Thor and his father, the all-powerful Odin. He's a mysterious figure, often relegated to the margins of mythological texts; yet, his very existence beckons us to dig deeper and inquire. Picture a dinner table where Odin, the father of gods, sits at the head, and Thor, the god of thunder, steals the limelight with his boisterous tales. Then there's Meili, sitting quietly—perhaps overlooked, but not insignificant.

The name Meili evokes curiosity. Translated from Old Norse, it means "the one who is a mile-stepper" or "the mile-great." Peculiar, isn't it? While we may not know exactly what this name implies, we are enticed to speculate. Could Meili be a god of distances, of boundaries, or perhaps even of journeys? Imagine him walking with a measured pace across vast landscapes, metaphorical or literal, marking the parameters between worlds or states of being.

Meili's scant references in mythology might not be a mere oversight but a feature, hinting at his role as a deity of the overlooked, the marginal, or perhaps the quietly influential. While the Norse pantheon is replete with tales of grandeur—of wars and epic quests—Meili might represent the elements of existence that are often in the background but are essential. Can you imagine him standing in the tranquil eye of the storm conjured by Thor, steadying it and providing balance? What an interesting counterpoint to his more exuberant sibling! While Thor might be tempestuous and immediate, Meili could be a figure of reflection and enduring stability.

Being Odin's son—ah, what a lineage—suggests that he could possess cosmic responsibilities, albeit less visible ones. The realm of the gods is well-balanced cosmic machinery, and who's to say Meili doesn't have a hand in maintaining that balance? It's a captivating thought: a god operating behind the scenes, quietly ensuring the universe remains in equilibrium.

And what of the fraternal relationship between Meili and Thor? While Thor hammers away, causing ripples across worlds, could Meili's less visible divine actions offer another facet of godhood—one that's less about might and more about subtlety, less about roaring thunder and more about the whispering winds?

Ullr

Ullr, often known as the god of skiing, archery, and hunting, occupies a unique place. Far from being a minor god, Ullr is, in fact, a compelling character deeply embedded in the traditions and survival tactics of ancient Scandinavia.

The harsh winters of the North transform the land itself into a demanding adversary. Here, skiing and archery evolve from mere sports into essential life skills. Ullr, as the god of these activities, assumes a mantle that far surpasses mere recreation. He is a mirror of the human struggle against nature's harshest elements and a divine mentor in the art of survival. Picture him gliding gracefully down snow-covered slopes, arrows hitting their marks flawlessly—an embodiment of mastery over the land's toughest challenges. This is Ullr: a god not just of sport but of the urgent, immediate necessities that come with life in a severe landscape.

But Ullr is not a deity solely defined by utility. His beauty, described in some texts as so astonishing that he appears to shine, adds nuance. He's not just a god of survival but also of elegance, of the beauty that can be found in the finesse of a well-aimed shot or perhaps even in the act of surviving against the odds.

Ullr's position within the divine family tree further enriches our understanding of him. As the son of the goddess Sif and the stepson of the mighty Thor, he is an amalgamation of different divine elements. It's as if he straddles two worlds: one of aesthetic refinement and one of raw, elemental force. In Ullr, we witness a marriage of Sif's gentle nurturing with Thor's dynamic power, creating a character of astonishing depth.

There is yet another aspect to consider: Ullr as the god invoked in duels. Dueling is not just a physical contest; it is a ritual steeped in ethics and specific rules. Here, Ullr emerges as a god who values skill over sheer force, precision over unchecked might, and moral conduct over aggression. Imagine two warriors calling upon Ullr before a duel, their eyes reflecting not just the anticipation of combat but a profound understanding of its ethical dimensions.

Vali

Vali, a god who embodies the very essence of targeted vengeance and swift justice, serves as a fascinating window into the values, ideas, and tensions that permeate the Norse cosmos.

Imagine being born into the world with a single, pressing mission. This describes Vali, whose very reason for existence revolves around avenging the death of Baldr, Odin's cherished son. Vali emerges not as a vulnerable infant but as a warrior in full form, bypassing childhood entirely. Within merely a day of his birth, Vali fulfills his solemn duty by killing Hodr, the unfortunate half-brother deceived by Loki into causing Baldr's death. In Vali, we encounter a deity whose existence represents not personal revenge but a larger concept of cosmic balance. The death of Baldr, the most adored among the Aesir, has severely disrupted the divine order. In avenging him, Vali restores a sense of justice—an essential component in Norse culture often expressed through blood feuds and duels.

Vali's swift metamorphosis from birth to a fully realized warrior serves as a manifestation of the relentless hand of fate, a concept deeply ingrained in Norse understanding. There is no room for error or the luxury of a childhood spent exploring and making mistakes. This can be viewed as an expression of Norse fatalism, mirrored in the work of the Norns, those mysterious beings who weave the destinies of gods and mortals alike. In a cosmos where destiny is tightly and unyieldingly woven, Vali stands as a potent symbol of the roles that even gods cannot escape.

However, let us not overlook the somber aspect of Vali's existence. The vengeance he exacts is indeed a familial matter—his mission results in the killing of his own half-brother, Hodr. In fulfilling his destiny, Vali embodies the dichotomy of justice and tragedy that marks the Aesir's complex family dynamics. Although he is a force of reckoning, he also perpetuates the cycle of violence that seems to haunt this divine family. It's as if Vali is caught in an intricate dance of justice and retribution, reflecting the complexities that characterize the very nature of justice within this mythical universe.

And then consider this: in many respects, Vali appears as the antithesis of Loki, the god of trickery whose cunning set the stage for Vali's birth. Where Loki is a master of chaos and unpredictability, Vali serves as a pillar of straightforwardness and resolution. Both are entangled in the unbreakable web of fate, acting as agents who, willingly or not, pave the way for the impending apocalypse known as Ragnarök.

Vili and Ve

Vili and Ve are two fascinating deities who play roles of cosmic significance. Their tale is intricately woven with that of their brother Odin. If we pause to consider each of them individually, we find an astonishing depth and interplay of characteristics that both mirror and enrich those of the Allfather.

Vili, whose name intriguingly translates to "will" or "desire," has the ethereal task of endowing humanity with consciousness, emotions, and intelligence. Picture him as the master architect of the internal landscapes that make us who we are. While Odin provides the breath that animates life and Ve graces us with form and sensory perception, it is Vili who adds the faculties that elevate life from mere existence to a realm of meaning and thought. One can think of Vili as the deity governing our emotional and intellectual inner world, the recesses where our unique individuality blossoms.

Now let's turn our gaze to Ve, whose name wonderfully translates to "sanctuary" or "home." How fitting for a deity who is the custodian of the external, material aspects of existence. It is Ve who provides the contours of the physical world, shaping not only humanity but also the universe at large. If Odin and Vili are preoccupied with matters of the mind and spirit, Ve is the god who champions the tangible, corporeal elements that make life not just an abstraction but a lived experience. In the Norse cosmos, Ve serves as a compelling reminder that divinity also resides in the material world we can touch and see. Odin, Vili, and Ve are not isolated entities but operate as a symphony, each bringing a different instrument to the cosmic orchestra. Odin, as the grand conductor, epitomizes wisdom, warcraft, and cosmic insight. Vili adds the melodies of emotion, will, and cognition, while Ve introduces the rhythms of the physical world, the corporeal reality. This forms a harmonious triad, each deity enriching the others, embodying a holistic understanding of existence that incorporates the spiritual, mental, and physical domains. Through them, Norse philosophy articulates a world where everything is interconnected, where the divine is not a monolithic entity but a complex, multi-layered essence.

They are co-creators, collaborators in the grand project of existence. This detail subtly hints at an egalitarian sensibility in Norse mythological thinking. No single deity bears the exclusive mantle for the creation of the world or the complexities of human life. Instead, it's a collective effort, a cosmic collaboration.

Vidar

Vidar, the son of Odin and the giantess Grid, is a remarkable blend of the divine Aesir and the elemental Jotunn. Often referred to as the "Silent God," Vidar is a deity of particular fascination, layered with characteristics that render him uniquely compelling.

Consider Vidar's extraordinary physical strength, even among gods. His magical shoe, an artifact made from the scraps of all the shoes ever created, is a piece of cosmic tailoring worth noting. This is no ordinary shoe; it is designed to give Vidar the leverage he needs during Ragnarök. When the time comes to avenge his father Odin, this very shoe will provide Vidar with the power to tear apart Fenrir. It's as though the shoe itself embodies focused retribution and long-awaited justice.

Now, step into the quiet realm of Vidar's silence, another fascinating layer of his personality. Unlike other gods, who may be more theatrical in their actions and words, Vidar is reserved, holding his peace until the moment is ripe. This could be viewed not merely as reticence but as a form of contemplative strategy. This nuanced characteristic adds incredible depth to Vidar, suggesting he is not just a figure of revenge but a deity who values restraint and thoughtful timing. His silence is not absence but a rich presence; it whispers of untapped power and a will held in potent reserve.

This inner quality manifests itself in the environment Vidar calls home—a place far removed from the bustling halls of gods and warriors, filled with brushwood and tall grasses. Such an unassuming yet resilient environment reflects Vidar's own nature: silent but immensely powerful. It's as though the land itself is biding its time, waiting for the right moment to reveal its hidden strength.

Vidar is not merely a god of brute force or quiet contemplation; he is a god of destiny. From the very moment of his birth, he is preordained for a singular act, a role from which he cannot escape. The act Vidar is fated to perform is more than just a family affair; it's a cosmic necessity. He is not merely avenging a father; he is contributing to the destruction and rebirth that shape the Norse universe. His vengeance serves both as an end and a new beginning, a cycle that aligns perfectly with the Norse understanding of a world in constant flux.

Mimir

The enigmatic Mimir is a figure that captures the essence of wisdom in its most sublime form. Neither wielding a sword nor sitting on a throne, he epitomizes intellectual pursuit and the labyrinthine nature of enlightenment. His tale is filled with paradoxes, serving as a poetic allegory of wisdom, sacrifice, and the dual-edged sword of knowledge.

Let's explore Mimir's primary trait—his incomparable wisdom. Mímir's Well, or Mímisbrunnr as it is traditionally called, is no ordinary pool of water but a repository of cosmic wisdom. Situated near the root of Yggdrasil that stretches into Jotunheim, the land of the giants, the well beckons with untold secrets. Every day, Mimir drinks from these enigmatic waters using the Gjallarhorn, thus imbibing its profound wisdom. This act is more than ritualistic; it symbolizes an unending quest for knowledge. Ah, the responsibility of guarding such a treasure must be immense! Mimir's wisdom came at a high cost during the Aesir-Vanir war, a cataclysmic conflict that claimed his life. His head was severed but found a second life when Odin preserved it with a delicate blend of herbs and magical incantations. The head continued to speak, offering invaluable counsel to Odin, who, even with all his wisdom, found himself in need of Mimir's unique insights. Here, we contemplate the philosophical dimensions of wisdom: can it transcend mortality? Is enlightenment an eternal journey?

The motif of sacrifice recurs in Mimir's tale, raising an intriguing point. Odin gave up an eye to partake of the well's wisdom. Both acts—Mimir's beheading and Odin's sacrifice—underline an elemental truth: true wisdom requires sacrifice. Mimir's very existence seems to serve as a cosmic enforcer of this principle of intellectual exchange.

Even as a disembodied head, Mimir is far from a passive character. Consider the invaluable advice he offers Odin, especially during the tumultuous moments leading to Ragnarök. It's as if he's suggesting that wisdom is not a static state but a dynamic and ongoing engagement with the intricacies of the cosmos.

Think of Mimir as a sort of cosmic bridge. His well is tied to Yggdrasil, the great tree that links all of reality. As a character who traverses realms—from his Aesir origin to his afterlife in Jotunheim—he suggests that wisdom is not merely an isolated virtue but a universal constant, a connecting thread in the tapestry of existence.

As we reflect on Mimir, we are reminded of the multifaceted nature of wisdom, which is intricately connected to sacrifice, to eternity, and to the endless cycle of learning and enlightenment.

Vanir Gods

The Vanir are enigmatic gods often overshadowed by the more warlike Aesir, yet they are equally captivating. Picture a lush landscape where nature is not merely a backdrop but a vibrant, living entity. In this realm, the Vanir gods reign. To simply label them as deities of fertility and prosperity would be akin to capturing a complex mosaic with a single brushstroke.

Consider their skill in diplomacy and reconciliation—a rather fascinating trait for gods, wouldn't you agree? While the Aesir might resolve conflicts through might and magic, the Vanir take a different approach. They are negotiators and harmonizers, serving as pillars of social cohesion. Their unique form of wisdom establishes them as mediators—figures who resolve disputes not by overpowering but by understanding.

Let's also discuss their distinct brand of wisdom, which is refreshingly pragmatic. These are gods who understand the complexities of farming and the unpredictable temperaments of the sea. This is the everyday wisdom of the Vanir, a wisdom tied to the earthly plane. If you find yourself dealing with immediate, tangible problems, it is to the Vanir that you would likely turn. Their wisdom is not based on abstract cosmic understanding but is deeply rooted in the immediate concerns of human life.

Contrast this with the Aesir, who are often preoccupied with questions of fate and the grand cosmic plan. The Vanir, you'll find, have a more cyclical view of existence. They perceive life as a wheel, endlessly turning through cycles of life, death, and rebirth. This perspective celebrates the rhythms of nature and understands the universe as an interconnected, ever-changing, yet ever-constant cycle. This viewpoint goes beyond mere nature worship to offer a profound understanding of the world.

As we delve into the depths of what makes the Vanir gods so compelling, we discover a unique lens through which to view divinity. This lens offers a vision of harmony, cyclical renewal, and a deeply nuanced understanding of prosperity and wisdom.

Gerda

Gerðr, often Anglicized as Gerda, is a figure who straddles realms. She is not a goddess but rather a Jotunn, a giantess. Yet her story and her attributes plunge us into the depths of complex subjects such as love, agency, and the intermingling of different worlds. When discussing her, we embark on an exploration of the intricate dance between power, choice, and emotional realities within the mythical landscape.

The moment Freyr lays eyes on Gerðr for the first time, infatuation strikes him instantly. This is not a fleeting attraction but a deep, desperate love that sets the stage for an intricate courtship. Here, Gerðr reveals herself as a woman with agency, a woman who sets conditions. When Freyr's servant Skírnir arrives as a messenger to propose marriage, Gerðr is not easily swayed. Consider the courage it takes to maintain one's autonomy when faced with tactics that hover dangerously close to threats. The intensity of Skírnir's actions should not be overlooked. He offers not just gifts but rune spells designed to forcibly tug at the strings of her will. This alone emphasizes Gerðr's remarkable inner strength and resilience. It's only when Skírnir darkens the proposal with a terrifying curse—one that would isolate her in a miserable existence—that Gerðr agrees to the union. Even in this, however, she is exercising her ability to choose within the boundaries set before her. Rather than rendering her powerless, this illustrates the often-complicated conditions under which we make choices.

Once married to Freyr, Gerðr undergoes a transformation. She steps into the role of a goddess of fertility but does so while carrying the untamed vigor of her Jotunn heritage. Here we witness a beautiful paradox: a Vanir god united with a giantess, the essence of fertility interwoven with primal forces, and love born from a labyrinth of desire, coercion, and calculated decisions.

Consider what her presence does to the Vanir pantheon, traditionally associated with fertility and prosperity. Gerðr infuses it with something untamed, something primal from her own lineage. The inclusion of her character lends a richer texture to the Vanir concepts, suggesting a divine landscape where the harmonious and the wild not only coexist but enrich one another.

Gullveig

The enigmatic Gullveig is a figure shrouded in veils of mystique and alluring ambiguity, her essence captured in fragments of ancient text, particularly in the "Völuspá" of the Poetic Edda. Many perceive her merely as a sorceress linked to greed and darker instincts, yet that view offers an incomplete portrait. She is not merely a character; she is a catalyst, an instigator who holds up a mirror to the darker recesses of the gods themselves, ultimately setting the stage for transformation and renewal.

To begin, let's decipher her name, shall we? "Gull" denotes gold, and "Veig" signifies an intoxicating drink or power. Her name almost foreshadows her role. When she sets foot in Asgard, she does more than merely visit; she triggers a cascade of events. Stabbed and burned three times, yet emerging anew each time, she embodies an uncanny resilience, a cycle of life and death in vivid contrast to the gods, who derive their own form of immortality from Iðunn's apples.

This cyclical transformation of Gullveig serves as more than a spectacle; it is a wake-up call to the gods. She acts as a mirror, reflecting their darker cravings for wealth and power. Through her, they come face-to-face with their own darker impulses. In a sense, she serves as the spark that ignites the volatile mixture of grievances and mistrust among the gods, leading to the cataclysmic Aesir-Vanir war. It's almost as if she pulls the rug out from under their feet, forcing them to confront issues they would rather ignore.

She is often equated with Heiðr, a volva or seeress skilled in the magical art of seidr. This magical discipline, laden with the potential to alter fate itself, is generally more closely aligned with the Vanir or even the Jotnar, the giants. Her association with this form of magic casts her as an outsider—someone who brings previously fringe elements into the epicenter of Asgard.

Gullveig is a multi-faceted enigma, embodying the complexities and dualities of existence itself. While some may view her as a disruptive force, she might just as well be seen as an embodiment of life's inescapable complexities. Greed, resilience, transformative power, and magical prowess do not exist as isolated aspects; they blend within her, producing a cocktail of traits that enriches the narrative and shakes the gods out of their complacency. Through her, we learn that disruption can serve as a catalyst for growth, forcing hidden issues into the open where they can be addressed and possibly leading to renewal.

Nerthus

Nerthus is a deity whose narrative we owe largely to the Roman historian Tacitus. Isn't it fascinating that her presence is recorded in the ancient pen strokes of a civilization not her own? Although often envisioned as the sister or perhaps the feminine echo of Njord, the Vanir god of the sea, Nerthus distinguishes herself as an entity in her own right. She embodies themes that resonate deeply within the human experience: fertility, agriculture, and most captivating of all, peace. She serves as an archetype of the Earth Mother, and her rites and rituals offer a window into how ancient Germanic societies viewed their intricate relationship with the natural world.

Imagine a sacred cart carrying Nerthus' effigy meandering through villages, serving not just as a display but as a bearer of peace and prosperity. During her procession, every weapon is sheathed, and the air fills with an aura of communal harmony. This is not the battlefield valor that characterizes war deities. Instead, Nerthus exerts her divine influence in a different way, through the cessation of conflict and the harmonization of society. One could even argue that her very arrival commands peace, like a sovereign whose mere presence compels obeisance.

However, one should not mistake her for a merely benign presence. Her worship carries its own somber notes. The slaves who ceremonially bathe her statue meet a watery end, drowned as part of the ritual. She is nurturing, yes, but also awe-inspiring, commanding a form of respect that veers into the realm of the fearsome. Nerthus embodies dualities; she is both a giver and a taker, a force of life and a harbinger of mortality. These contrasting layers add intriguing complexity to her character.

Consider the act of bathing her statue not as simple purification but as an annual regeneration. The fields that feed us lie fallow to renew their fertility; rivers flow back to their sources in endless loops. In a similar manner, Nerthus experiences her cyclical renewal, underscoring her profound symbiosis with the natural world and the perpetual cycle of giving and taking life.

A curious aspect of Nerthus is her silence. She doesn't speak; her will is interpreted through a priest who accompanies her. This silent forcefulness could be seen as a reflection of the Earth's mysterious yet omnipresent power. The Earth doesn't require human language to communicate its wisdom; its mere existence is a statement. In Nerthus, we find a deity who is both intimate and distant: a nurturer that connects closely with human communities yet retains an otherworldly enigma that makes her profoundly divine, beyond the grasp of everyday understanding.

Odr

Imagine being known more for your absence than your presence. Such is the enigmatic figure of Odr, forever tied in matrimony to Freyja, one of Norse mythology's most formidable goddesses. While it's tempting to focus solely on Freyja's dazzling persona, Odr should not be overlooked. He offers a compelling narrative steeped in themes of love, loss, and yearning that stretch the bounds of both earthly and divine realms.

Odr is perpetually "elsewhere." His wanderlust defines his essence. Although he is often away on journeys to undefined lands, Freyja weeps tears of red gold for him. The reasons behind his ceaseless voyages are veiled in mystery, but they are potent enough to separate him from a goddess renowned for her unmatched beauty and power. Here, we glimpse the timeless essence of human—and perhaps divine—curiosity: the search for something ineffable, something that even a union with a deity cannot fully satisfy.

Odr's name is not merely a name; it's a portal to a more expansive concept. Linguistically connected to "Odhinn," or Odin, the god of wisdom and poetic inspiration, Odr is also a seeker. But while Odin's quests are wide-ranging and often demand a sacrificial price, Odr's voyages seem to focus more on emotional landscapes. And don't think that his absence leaves a void; it serves more as a catalyst. In her longing for him, Freyja becomes a wanderer herself, her travels reflecting the eternal archetype of the divine feminine in search of union with the divine masculine. In this way, Odr serves as a fulcrum, a gravitational point around which Freyja finds her own complexity and nuance.

Sometimes there are whispers that Odr appears under different names, adopting multiple forms much like Odin, although less explicitly. This suggests the transformative essence of quests, illustrating how the journey itself can be an alchemy that changes you, from your experiences down to your very identity.

It's important to note that Odr is draped in ambiguity. His narrative is more hinted at than explicitly laid out, rendering him an elusive figure. Yet perhaps it is this very elusiveness that endows him with universal relevance. Through Odr, we encounter the tension between our obligations and our individual quests, the inevitable dichotomy of love and separation, and the ever-present allure of the unknown that pulls at the deepest recesses of our souls.

Freyr

Freyr—a deity who occupies a significant position at the confluence of what the ancient Norse considered the fundamental pillars of life: fertility, prosperity, and peace. As a member of the Vanir clan, gods closely associated with these domains, Freyr has a portfolio that resists easy categorization. From overseeing agricultural bounty to ensuring matrimonial happiness, his influence provides a vivid portrait of a society's values: a harmonious blend of physical sustenance and spiritual contentment.

Now, let's explore some of the symbols associated with Freyr, shall we? Consider Skíðblaðnir, a ship that can be folded like a piece of cloth when not in use—a truly magnificent artifact. This ship is not merely a splendid piece of divine engineering; it also serves as a metaphor for Freyr's jurisdiction over wealth and prosperity. Just as Skíðblaðnir can expand its bounds to accommodate an endless number of warriors, so too does Freyr's largesse extend across various domains, showering blessings that manifest in myriad forms.

But there's more—consider his sword. This is not just a weapon but also an emblem of his power. In a tale revealing his multifaceted nature, Freyr relinquishes his sword to win the affections of Gerðr. This act is illuminating. While other gods in the Norse pantheon might relish their martial prowess, Freyr willingly sacrifices a form of his power to pursue a different kind of richness. In this context, he takes on the roles of lover, peacemaker, and indeed, diplomat, prioritizing emotional and spiritual integrity over martial might.

Freyr's relationship with Gerðr is not merely a romantic escapade; it serves as cosmic mediation. In Norse tradition, gods and giants embody contrasting forces: one symbolizes order and civilization, the other represents the wild unpredictability of nature. Their union, therefore, creates a harmonious blend of these cosmic elements, emphasizing Freyr's role as a deity of growth—a phenomenon that is both structured and serendipitous.

Freyr's character finds its most poignant expression in the prophecy of

Ragnarök. Even knowing that he will face this apocalyptic event without his magical sword, Freyr confronts Surtr, the fearsome fire giant, in a battle of tragic proportions. In this moment, Freyr becomes the quintessential tragic hero, facing an inevitable fate with both valor and equanimity, reflecting the Norse culture's deep-seated acceptance of destiny.

Freyja

Freyja, a goddess who intriguingly refuses to be confined to a single realm or set of attributes, is the daughter of Njord and sister to Freyr. However, her domain extends far beyond mere fertility. Freyja embodies such disparate yet intimately connected facets of existence as love, lust, beauty, sensuality, war, and even death. As we explore her many aspects, we find a character intricately woven from diverse threads, echoing the full spectrum of human experiences and sentiments. Freyja reigns over matters closest to the human heart and hearth. She is not merely a symbol but the epitome of romantic and sexual desires that have driven stories and tragedies throughout human history. Gods and giants alike find themselves smitten by her charm, reflecting the potent allure she emanates. In the sphere of love and sexuality, she presents a harmonious duality, capturing both the spiritual and the corporeal facets of these human experiences. Freyja is not solely devoted to affairs of love or domestic life. Astonishingly, she is also a goddess of war, riding a chariot drawn by two giant cats—emblems of her fierce independence and untamed spirit. After the clamor of battle has faded, half of the fallen warriors find their way to her hall, Sessrúmnir, while the other half go to Odin's Valhalla. In this role, she disrupts the conventional image of what feminine deities should embody, beautifully blending the characteristics of nurturing and destruction. She is the master of a form of magic known as "seidr," which involves the arcane arts of divination and destiny alteration. Even Odin learns this craft from her. Through her mastery of magic, Freyja adds another layer of depth and enigma, hinting at elusive aspects of existence that continue to elude human comprehension. Her magic is both a tool and a talent, influencing the world's events in ways both overt and subtle. The intriguing tale of Freyja's Brísingamen, a necklace of extraordinary beauty, should not be overlooked. The story of how she acquires it is a study in the complexities of desire, sacrifice, and individual agency. Freyja makes a conscious choice to trade her favors for this exquisite piece, and in doing so, she brings to light the sacrifices and negotiations we all make in the pursuit of what we long for. The necklace itself becomes not just an adornment but a multi-layered emblem of her autonomy, power, and the consequences of choice. Let's consider one of Freyja's most mysterious attributes: her ability to move between worlds. With her feathered cloak that transforms her into a falcon, Freyja is a wanderer not confined to Asgard alone. Whether she's in pursuit of her lost husband Odr or venturing into unknown realms for motives known only to her, Freyja symbolizes the eternal quest for knowledge and understanding, for a sense of wholeness that perhaps all beings seek.

Njord

Njord, a god who stands in stark contrast to others, originates from Vanaheim, the home of the Vanir gods. He governs realms such as the sea, seafaring, wealth, and, of course, abundance. Through Njord, we not only grasp how the Norse people perceived the ocean—a vast expanse that could be both generous and perilous—but we also learn what they deemed essential for a fulfilling life: prosperity, tranquility, and family bonds.

The sea is an ever-present force in the lives of Norse communities. It serves as a source of food, a highway for exploration, and a setting fraught with danger. In navigating this complexity, who better to turn to than Njord? He has the power to temper the capricious seas and winds, ensuring safer passage for sailors. Whether you're a fisherman hoping for an abundant catch or a trader seeking prosperous deals, paying homage to Njord could tip the scales in your favor. But the ocean is not simply a domain of economic opportunity; under Njord's oversight, it also becomes a realm of moral and spiritual richness.

Another often-overlooked aspect of Njord is his association with wealth. It's not solely about material riches, although that is part of it. Njord embodies a more nuanced concept of prosperity, one that includes the virtues of peace and harmonious living. When we speak of wealth in the context of Njord, we're discussing a life that is not just materially affluent but also spiritually content.

As the father of Freyr and Freyja—figures linked to fertility and love—Njord already plays an important role. However, it's his marriage to the giantess Skadi that reveals another facet of his character. These two beings come from different worlds: he loves the sea, while she is enamored with mountains. Although this union was initially born out of necessity to compensate Skadi for her father's death, it is not devoid of efforts to find common ground. Though the marriage does not endure, the endeavor reflects Njord's inherent qualities as a diplomat and peacemaker. Here, he embodies the compromises, adjustments, and occasional discomforts that often characterize familial and societal peace.

Let it be clear: Njord's realm is not some utopian landscape devoid of challenges. The sea has its moods, and peace is a delicate flower that requires nurturing. In this context, Njord becomes not a god who removes obstacles but one who provides the means to navigate through them. He grants favorable winds, offers the prospect of a bountiful catch, and bestows the wisdom to foster peace.

The Aesir And Vanir War

The celestial drama of the Aesir-Vanir War is not just a tale of gods and conflict; it's an intriguing narrative that helped shape the foundation of the Norse cosmos and the pantheon of deities.

In one corner, we have the Aesir—deities of war, sky, and wisdom, captained by none other than Odin himself. They make their home in Asgard and are often considered the more dominant of the two divine families. In the opposing corner are the Vanir, inhabitants of Vanaheim, whose dominion extends over fertility, prosperity, and the natural world. Each family has its own unique rituals and powers, setting the stage for a conflict that will echo throughout time.

The catalyst for this war remains somewhat ambiguous. However, one popular account tells of Gullveig, who was not just mistreated but also speared and burned three times by the Aesir, only to resurrect each time. Such an audacious act set the stage for a full-scale divine war.

Unlike mortal conflicts, which often culminate in the crushing defeat of one party, this celestial war took a different course. Exhausted and worn from battle, neither side could claim a decisive victory. Both sustained substantial losses, creating an atmosphere that made peace not just desirable but essential. Thus, a truce was negotiated, sealed in a most unusual fashion: both divine families spat into a cauldron, from which was born Kvasir, the wisest of all beings. His legacy would later contribute to the creation of the Mead of Poetry.

Tangible changes followed. A hostage exchange occurred: Hoenir and Mimir were sent to Vanaheim, while Njord and his children, Freyr and Freyja, moved to Asgard. This led to a fascinating cultural assimilation and intermingling of divine powers. Freyr and Freyja, originally Vanir gods, were so warmly embraced in Asgard that they became integral parts of the Aesir tradition.

Hoenir, sent to Vanaheim, proved to be rather indecisive and dependent on Mimir for counsel. This ultimately led to Mimir's unfortunate beheading—a moment so significant it spawned its own set of myths, including Mimir becoming a wise advisor to Odin from beyond the grave.

The conflict's aftermath even influenced the architectural designs of Asgard. A wall was erected, with some assistance from a giant, to bolster the realm's defenses. The Aesir and Vanir were formally unified into a single pantheon, although each retained their own unique set of skills and responsibilities.

The Jötnar: The Wilderness Tribe

The Jötnar, the giants, don't be too quick to label them as mere adversaries of the gods from the Aesir and Vanir families. Intricately tied to the forces of nature, they're ancient entities that embody both chaos and wisdom. By examining their nuanced portrayals, we're given a fascinating window into the Norse understanding of the delicate balance between order and chaos, and the intertwining of culture and nature.

The Jötnar as the essential forces that give shape to the very cosmos—ice, fire, storms—these are their domains. What a magnificent paradox they embody! They are creators and destroyers in one, giving form to the universe even as they pose continual challenges to its ordered realms. This duality serves as an eloquent expression of the complex relationship between these giants and the gods: both cooperation and conflict, creation and dissolution.

Many among the Jötnar possess wisdom so ancient and fundamental that even the gods turn to them for knowledge. It's not wisdom as we commonly understand it; it's something far more elemental. Imagine understanding the world from the perspective of its foundational forces; this is the wisdom that the Jötnar offer, insights profoundly anchored in the rhythms and cycles of nature. It's a wisdom that transcends the gods' more anthropocentric viewpoints The Jötnar not solely as antagonists to the gods. Such an interpretation would be an unfortunate simplification. It's fascinating, is it not, that many gods themselves have mothers who are Jötnar? Moreover, relationships and even marriages occur between these giants and gods. Think of Loki, a complex character born from a Jötunn lineage, who wanders freely between the realms of gods and giants. Or consider Skadi, a jötunn who becomes an Aesir by marrying Njord. These exchanges tell us that the boundary separating the gods and giants is not as impermeable as one might think. Instead, it suggests a more fluid continuum between these two realms.

The Jotnars role in the Ragnarök, will align themselves against the gods, leading to destruction and yet, intriguingly, to rebirth. This dual role once again highlights their function as agents of both termination and genesis. The world will be submerged, echoing the primordial chaos from which it emerged, only to rise again, renewed and reborn.

Ymir

Ymir, an incredible primordial figure in Norse mythology, serves as a crossroads of creation and annihilation. He is both the source of elemental chaos and the foundation for cosmic order. Ymir is not merely a character in a tale; he is a concept, an embodiment of the raw matter that forms the backbone of existence. What a magnificent, multifaceted figure he is, offering invaluable insights into not only the birth of the Norse world but also the very principles that sustain it.

Ymir emerges from Ginnungagap, the great void where fire and ice intertwine. He is almost like an elemental equation resulting from this cosmic interaction, encapsulating the endless possibilities of a nature yet to be tamed. To say he is an individual would be limiting; he is more accurately described as a living manifestation of raw, untamed nature.

The paradox Ymir represents in the act of world creation is intriguing. On one hand, he serves as a foundational force—his very being offers the raw materials needed for the world to come into existence. On the other hand, consider the sheer chaos residing within him, a tumultuous essence that must be tamed or even dismantled to forge a stable world. Here, our focus shifts to Odin and his brothers, Vili and Ve. Their role is not as simple as merely slaying Ymir; it is a transformational act that turns chaos into order, a grand cosmic drama that is as beautiful as it is brutal.

Ymir is not a passive cog in this wheel of creation. What often goes unnoticed is Ymir's own intrinsic agency, his dynamic role as a natural force that gives birth to the lineage of frost giants. Even in death, Ymir's influence does not wane; it continues through his descendants, a potent lineage that perennially challenges the reign of the Aesir gods. Ymir's essence seems to flow into the world, absorbed into its many facets. In a manner of speaking, he never truly dies; he merely transforms, his spirit scattering to infuse the world and its inhabitants.

Surtr

Surtr, the fiery giant, stands as the guardian of the realm of fire, Muspelheim. He is a figure so awe-inspiring that his sword of flame outshines even the sun. However, Surtr is not merely a villain in the story; he is a cosmic entity with a pivotal role in both the world's end and its rebirth.

If you closely consider Surtr's role, it becomes evident that fire is not merely a part of his form but also a mirror reflecting his larger function. Fire is a paradoxical element. On one hand, it destroys, reducing everything to ashes; on the other, it purifies,

paving the way for a new reality to emerge from the remnants of the old. In Surtr, this elemental paradox takes on flesh and form. The flames he wields can obliterate the cosmos, but they can also set the stage for a brand-new world to rise.
Unlike other giants in Norse mythology, who display a diverse range of characteristics from wisdom to cunning, Surtr seems almost single-mindedly focused on his role in Ragnarök. Exercise caution: labeling him as an embodiment of evil would be an oversimplification. He represents something more complex—a cycle, an eternal loop of death and rebirth. Surtr stands at its pivotal moment, the crucial turning point from one state to another.
Consider the sheer singularity of Surtr's purpose. Compared to the gods and other giants, who often become entangled in webs of strategy, negotiation, and intricate motives, Surtr is refreshingly uncomplicated. He doesn't deliberate; he doesn't bargain. He simply exists, and he acts, a force of nature that is as unyielding as it is impartial.
During the events of Ragnarök, Surtr sets the world tree Yggdrasil aflame, igniting a fire that engulfs all realms. From these very ashes, a rejuvenated world rises, emerging from the sea, ready to harbor new lives and narratives. Thus, while he may be a force of destruction, he is also a catalyst for creation.

Jord

Jord, the Earth Giantess, is also known by names such as Fjorgyn or Hlódyn. She embodies the very ground we walk upon, the hills that grace landscapes, and the intricate network of caverns that wind their way deep into the planet. Intriguingly, she is not merely an elemental being but also a celestial one—Thor's own mother—acting as a bridge between the realms of gods and mortals.

Jord, whose name translates to "Earth," carries a meaning as palpable as the soil we till and the rocks we quarry. She brings the world of mythology into the tangible, the corporeal. Think of her as a linchpin of stability and solidity, the eternal nurturer who sustains not only gods but also mere mortals.

When considering Jord as a mother, it is necessary to extend our gaze beyond her divine son, Thor. She is the mother of all beings—plant, animal, and human—that call Earth home. The fertility of the soil, the towering grace of trees—all are silent hymns sung in her honor. Although her presence may not be as overt as that of other mythological figures, it exists, woven into the fabric of existence. Each harvest, each mineral, and each geological formation serves as a testament to her.

She tends not to feature prominently in the theatrical dramas and epic struggles that populate the pages of Norse mythology. Instead, she exists as a sort of cosmic bedrock, a stable foundation on which all these dramatic narratives unfold. This characteristic could also be interpreted as a symbolic representation of Earth's impartiality. Like a silent observer, Earth provides and sustains, indifferent to the squabbles and conflicts among its inhabitants.

At first glance, Jord's seeming passivity could be construed as a lack of dynamism, especially when compared to more active figures in the mythological landscape. However, the Earth she embodies is anything but a meek entity. It is a titanic force brimming with dualities—life and death, creation and destruction. The very same Earth that causes volcanoes to erupt and earthquakes to rupture landscapes is also the one that gently nurtures seeds into blossoming life. Through Jord, we encounter the manifold complexities that make Earth not just a nurturing mother but also a formidable force.

Skadi

Amid frozen landscapes, we encounter Skadi, a figure who defies simplistic interpretations. A master huntress and skier, she embodies the untamed qualities of nature and winter. Skadi challenges the typical narratives that often cast giants as adversaries of the gods.

Her story resembles a riveting saga, fueled by an insatiable quest for justice. Her father, Thjazi, met his end at the hands of the gods. In response, Skadi marches into Asgard, not with a white flag, but fully armed, determined to avenge her father's death. This is our first glimpse into her character—a resolute, fearless woman, and a force to be reckoned with.

However, the tale takes an unexpected twist. Instead of the clamor of battle, we hear the whispers of diplomacy. Skadi marries Njord, the sea god, in a symbolic union meant to harmonize two disparate realms—Jotunheim's rugged terrain and Asgard's celestial landscapes, where land and sea are intertwined. But even myths are not free from the complexities of marital life. Skadi, a daughter of snow and ice, finds herself out of sorts in Njord's balmy, maritime realm. Njord, in turn, finds himself equally ill-suited for Skadi's icy domain. Eventually, they part ways, revealing Skadi's deeply ingrained unwillingness to compromise her essence for the sake of peace.

The mountains, the snow, the icy wilderness—these are not merely backdrops to Skadi's life; they are aspects of her very identity. She embodies what the Norse termed "Öndurdís," or ski-goddess, reflecting not just her skiing prowess but also her profound affinity for her natural environment. She epitomizes survival, deeply attuned to the brutal yet majestic cycles of life and death that dictate the rhythm of her frosty world.

One can't help but marvel at the labyrinthine facets of Skadi's character. She is driven by the pursuit of justice for her father, yet she opts for negotiation over retribution with the gods. Her nature, akin to the landscapes she inhabits, is breathtaking in its beauty but unforgiving in its harshness. This duality sets her apart as a multi-dimensional persona who cannot be easily pigeonholed or dismissed.

Heroes and Legends

Let us journey back in time, across stories so compelling and so rich in valor and imagination that they continue to captivate us today, much like an intricately carved runestone enduring the test of time. We encounter figures of such grandeur and monumental heroism that they become archetypes in their own right. These characters are woven so seamlessly into the cultural fabric that they remain beloved, not only in their native Scandinavia but also far beyond its borders.

Ragnar Lodbrok

Into the 9th century, we encounter a figure so magnetic and so brimming with audacity that he is revered as a paragon of Viking valor. Enter Ragnar Lodbrok, or as he is delightfully known, "Ragnar Hairy Breeches." Picture him embarking on his raid into France in 845 A.D., an escapade so audacious that it forever sealed his standing, not merely as a military leader, but as a hero who occupies a sacrosanct space in the annals of legends.

But Ragnar is not merely a blade-wielding warrior. Consider also his domestic sphere. His marriage to Lagertha, the iconic shieldmaiden, speaks of a man who understood the virtues of partnership and valor in all realms of life. This same Ragnar was also the esteemed father of sons whose names evoke awe and curiosity: Bjorn Ironside, Ivar the Boneless, and Halfdan Ragnarsson—each a saga unto himself.

His life, like a twisting Norse saga, holds its portions of sorrow. The haunting scene of his demise, a pit filled with venomous serpents, came courtesy of the King of Northumbria. Captured in the 13th-century narrative "The Tale of Ragnar's Sons," this episode has spawned numerous retellings that contribute to the rich tapestry that is Ragnar's enduring legacy.

Even in the face of historical ambiguity, where solid proof of his existence becomes elusive, the tale of Ragnar continues to be a wellspring of inspiration. Books, movies, and television series all bear testament to the undying fascination we hold for this iconic figure. Ragnar Lodbrok transcends the boundary between history and myth, capturing our collective imagination and making us all, in a way, part of his ongoing saga.

Björn Ironside

Bjorn Ironside commands our attention not merely as the offspring of the illustrious Ragnar Lodbrok, but also as a Norse chieftain and naval commander of prodigious repute. His military expeditions into the Mediterranean basin were nothing short of extraordinary, rightfully etching his name alongside those of history's greatest Viking luminaries. Consider him the founding ruler of the Munso dynasty. Indeed, this is a man whose footprint on history is

unmistakable, shaping narratives that have endured for centuries.
The saying goes that the apple doesn't fall far from the tree. The tale of young Bjorn launching a successful raid in northern France, alongside Hastein, hints at a sense of adventurism inherited from his legendary father, Ragnar. Yet Bjorn harbored ambitions that extended beyond familial legacy. Enraptured by tales of Rome's opulence, he aspired to conquer this epitome of civilization himself. One episode particularly captures the audacious ingenuity of Bjorn Ironside. Let us journey to the city of Luni, near the renowned Pisa. Mistakenly believing he had arrived at Rome, Bjorn concocted a stratagem of breathtaking audacity: he feigned his own death and allowed himself to be carried into the city in a coffin. Like a phantom, he sprang to life at the opportune moment, arming his companions who were concealed nearby. What followed was a masterstroke of martial skill; they fought their way to the city gate, allowing their Norse comrades to pour in and take the city.
The capture of Luni stands not merely as a footnote in history, but as a story that lends gravitas to his reputation as one of the most respected leaders of the Viking Age.

Beowulf

Beowulf, a Geatish warrior, emerges as a paragon of courage and virtue in an epic that explores the complexities of duty, honor, and the inevitable passage of time. In Heorot, the grand hall of King Hrothgar in Denmark—a place beset by a menacing creature of darkness known as Grendel—Beowulf first steps onto the stage, immediately distinguished by daring audacity. This is a man who chooses to face Grendel unarmed, deeming the creature unworthy of the grace of a blade. Such a decision is not merely a testament to his physical prowess; it reveals the contours of a mind steadfast in its heroic calling.
Returning to his native Geatland, Beowulf ascends to the throne, ruling with wisdom born from his prior experiences. What makes him an object of endless fascination is his evolution over time. Unlike eternally youthful heroes of other legends, Beowulf ages, matures, and must adapt to new kinds of challenges. Picture an older Beowulf, his face etched with the wisdom and woes of years, confronting a dragon that imperils his kingdom. This is not the impulsive youth but a seasoned king who comprehends the full magnitude of his kingly duties.
The clash with the dragon is a moment loaded with profound symbolism. Here, we witness the culmination of a life's quest, the pinnacle of Beowulf's enduring struggle with his own mortality. He slays the dragon, but pays the ultimate price, losing his own life. His end is not a defeat but the epitome of his life philosophy: to live valiantly, to act honorably, and to safeguard the well-being of his people until his final breath.
Beowulf is a character of extraordinary complexity. In his youth, he is driven by a desire for glory, a hunger to etch his name into the annals of heroism. Yet, as he ages, this urge is transmuted into a more nuanced form of bravery, one governed by duty and a recognition of the fragility of human affairs.

His reverence for King Hrothgar reflects a profound understanding of kinship and governance, a prelude to his own rule. His interactions with his warriors, most notably Wiglaf during the dragon encounter, illuminate the high standards of courage and fidelity he both exhibits and expects.

Sigmund

Sigmund, a figure shaped by fate and divine design, hails from the illustrious Völsung clan. He embodies a blend of valor and tragedy, making him a symbol of the implacable force of destiny that so dominates Norse cosmology.

The moment that catapults Sigmund into the limelight is poetic in its potency: he extracts the sword Gram from the tree Barnstokkr, a feat akin to touching the divine. This is no ordinary tree; it is one where the god Odin had personally lodged the sword. Here, we do not merely witness an act of physical might; we glimpse a soul chosen by the gods themselves, destined for greatness yet marred by the complications that accompany such divine favor.

However, Sigmund's life is deeply human, stitched together by complex relationships. Consider his rapport with his sister Signy, entangled as it is with honor and a quest for revenge against their family's nemesis, King Siggeir. This relationship poses unflinching questions about loyalty, sacrifice, and the murky decisions one is sometimes compelled to make in the name of righteousness.

Sigmund's story also takes us into shadowy corners of human morality when he, rather tragically, ends up marrying his own daughter. This grim turn of events, orchestrated by his sister to perpetuate the pure Völsung lineage, does not render Sigmund a passive victim. Instead, it encapsulates him in a labyrinth of ethical ambiguities, painting his life in nuanced shades of gray rather than stark black and white.

Let's pause to consider Sigmund's fatal meeting with Odin who, in the guise of a mere beggar, appears during Sigmund's ultimate battle. The shattering of Gram against Odin's spear is not just a turning point; it serves as an allegory of the limitations that gods and fate impose on human endeavors. Sigmund, despite his immense courage and strength, is not exempt from the edicts of destiny.

Even in his end, Sigmund finds a sort of redemption. His son Sigurd inherits Gram, now reforged, and carries forth the Völsung name. What was once a broken sword and a symbol of Sigmund's unfulfilled destiny becomes a beacon for future glory and hope.

Sigurd

Sigurd, or Siegfried as he is known in other traditions, has a story that is not just an adventurous tale but also a complex emotional and philosophical odyssey weaving through themes of destiny, heroism, and the intricate relationships that shape our lives.

Born to Sigmund, a hero of tragic glory, Sigurd inherits a dual legacy perfectly embodied in his father's reforged sword, Gram. This is not merely a blade of immense power; it is an iconic symbol of the burdens and blessings of his lineage. His early education occurs under the tutelage of Regin, his foster father. Here, Regin serves the dual role of mentor in arts both martial and intellectual, albeit with ulterior motives that involve a cursed treasure and a dragon named Fafnir, who is, curiously enough, Regin's transformed brother.

Let's pause to consider Sigurd's confrontation with Fafnir, a defining point in his life journey. Brandishing Gram and guided by none other than Odin in disguise, Sigurd not only slays the fearsome dragon but also bathes in its blood to gain invulnerability and consumes its heart to understand the language of birds. These actions transform Sigurd from a mere mortal warrior into a man touched by divine destiny, marked for extraordinary ventures.

Upon acquiring this newfound wisdom, Sigurd discerns Regin's treacherous intentions. Rather than falling victim to the plot, he takes charge of his destiny, kills Regin, and claims both the accursed treasure and the fateful ring, Andvaranaut. Sigurd encounters Brynhildr, a Valkyrie of immense wisdom and valor, establishing a relationship that adds nuanced layers to his character. Their love is not born of superficial attraction but is an alliance of minds and souls.

Yet, this is where the fabric of Sigurd's tale gathers its most tragic folds. Influenced by a love potion, he marries Gudrun, leading to a sequence of devastating betrayals and heartbreak. It is as if Sigurd becomes a puppet in a theater of cosmic irony, where he is manipulated by forces beyond his control, ensnared in the labyrinth of societal expectations and familial obligations.

Tragically, his life comes to an end in a tangled web of misunderstandings and jealousies involving Brynhildr and Gudrun, leading to his ultimate betrayal and death. Even in death, however, the echo of Sigurd's life reverberates through time. His son with Gudrun carries on the family's legacy.

Mythological Creatures in Norse Paganism

Comprising nine worlds, Norse cosmology doesn't merely play host to an array of gods and goddesses; it also teems with a multitude of mythological creatures. While it's tempting to imagine these beings solely as menacing figures lurking in the shadows, the Norse mythological landscape is far more nuanced. Just as in our own natural world, creatures here may evoke awe or fear, yet many are neither evil nor malicious. Some even possess benevolent or neutral characteristics. The presence of terrifying entities does indeed add darker hues to the palette that makes this mythology endlessly fascinating.

The corpus of Old Norse texts mentions an extensive list of creatures, far too many to delve into in detail within this brief exploration. However, let us guide you closer to some of the more iconic inhabitants that have captured human imagination for centuries.

Norns

Imagine standing at the edge of the Well of Urd, nestled beneath the roots of Yggdrasil. There, you find three enigmatic figures engaged in an act so fundamental that it shapes the very framework of existence. These are the Norns: Urd, Verdandi, and Skuld, figures of such gravity that even gods and mortals must bow before the destiny they weave.

Urd, often associated with the past, is usually considered the eldest of the three. In her hands lie the threads of all that has been, a reservoir of wisdom accumulated through hindsight and historical understanding. She is akin to a wise elder who shapes the framework that governs the unfolding of the present and the future.

Turn your attention to Verdandi, the emblem of the present. She is the dynamic force where the threads of the past gain tangible form. If Urd provides the framework, Verdandi is the stage where the drama unfolds, a realm buzzing with action and decision-making. The immediate 'now' springs to life under her touch. She captures the essence of each moment, fraught with the dynamism and uncertainty that define our current realities.

Skuld, responsible for the future, curiously bears a name also tied to the concept of 'debt.' This could imply that the future is a ledger of sorts, shaped by the actions and choices of both the past and present. Skuld's domain is an intriguing nebula of potentialities, a place that fuels our collective anxieties and hopes as we ponder what is yet to come.

What's captivating is how these figures embody a harmonious paradox. They are not mere executors of an immutable fate; they maintain a delicate equilibrium between predestination and free will. While actions can be performed and decisions made in Verdandi's present, they are all set against Urd's past and directed toward Skuld's myriad futures. Yet, the final tapestry they weave is often something that neither gods nor mortals can predict or alter. Their responsibility is not confined to individual fates alone; even cosmic events fall within their purview. Deities themselves seek counsel from the Norns, a striking testament to their role as the ultimate arbiters of wisdom and destiny. As caretakers of Yggdrasil, they do more than merely shape fate; they nurture the universe itself, reinforcing their intricate role in the cyclical rhythms of time and existence.

Níðhǫggr

Níðhǫggr, also known as Nidhogg, is a unique being often characterized as a dragon or serpent. This creature dwells in shadowy seclusion near the roots of Yggdrasil. At first glance, you might be tempted to view Níðhǫggr as an embodiment of malevolence because it continuously gnaws at the roots of Yggdrasil. Such an act, ostensibly destructive, threatens not only the World Tree but also the entire cosmos it supports. Indeed, Níðhǫggr represents elemental forces aiming to dissolve structures and usher in chaos. However, this gnawing also serves another purpose: it opens the door to renewal. As the creature erodes the old, it makes space for the new, much like forest fires that consume dead wood to make way for new life. In this sense, Níðhǫggr plays an indispensable role in the ongoing cycles of decay and rebirth central to Norse cosmology.

There is more—a layer that adds a morbid yet philosophically intriguing nuance to this creature. Níðhǫggr is also said to feast on the corpses of the dishonorable dead, those who have met their end without honor. While this may seem gruesome, consider it as a purification process. By consuming those who died in disgrace, the dragon effectively cleanses the world of their malign influence.

Its abode near the roots of Yggdrasil places it in indirect contact with other entities like the Norns, who weave the destiny of all beings, as well as creatures such as the eagle perched atop the tree and Ratatoskr, the squirrel that darts along the trunk. This forms a complex ecosystem where Níðhǫggr's destructive activities are counterbalanced by the constructive actions of these other beings, thereby maintaining a delicate equilibrium in the cosmos.

Finally, come Ragnarök, Níðhǫggr takes center stage. This creature breaks free from its isolated existence to partake in cataclysmic events that will reshape the universe. It is as if the lid containing chaos is suddenly lifted, and Níðhǫggr emerges as a potent symbol of forces that can no longer be held back. Although accounts may differ on the particulars, the prevailing thought remains: Níðhǫggr, in unleashing its full potential, coincides with the great dissolution of cosmic order.

Huginn and Muninn

Huginn and Muninn are the two ravens who enjoy a special rapport with Odin. These are not mere decorative companions but extensions of Odin's own will and intellect. Huginn translates to "Thought," and Muninn stands for "Memory," indicating the crucial cerebral realms they govern. Huginn serves as the manifestation of Odin's analytical and curious nature. When sent across the nine realms— from the familiar terrain of Midgard to the distant reaches of the cosmos— Huginn's mission is to observe and gather knowledge. Think of him as the epitome of intellectual exploration, embodying the ceaseless urge for understanding that so defines Odin. Being a raven, Huginn also embodies certain attributes cherished in Norse culture: intelligence, resourcefulness, and the capability to navigate intricate landscapes. Huginn symbolizes Odin's intellectual pursuits, including curiosity, rigorous analysis, and the relentless quest for wisdom.

Now let's shift our focus to Muninn. As "Memory," he performs a role that is both complementary and fundamentally distinct. Muninn serves as the keeper of context and significance. It's important to remember that, in Norse thought, memory is an active function. Without Muninn, the data gathered by Huginn would be like floating debris, devoid of any anchoring context. Muninn provides that sense of continuity, tying new information back to Odin's past experiences and accumulated wisdom. Through him, Odin retains not only a sense of identity and purpose but also a rich backdrop of cultural and historical knowledge against which new experiences gain meaning.

Each day, Huginn and Muninn fly out into the world, scouring the nine realms for fresh insights. In the evening, they return to perch on Odin's shoulders, whispering their discoveries into his ears. This intimate daily ritual illustrates not only Odin's insatiable quest for wisdom but also his own limitations. Even the Allfather is not all-knowing. Huginn and Muninn act as his eyes and ears in the universe, augmenting his cognitive faculties. Through their expeditions, Odin continuously refreshes his understanding of a world in perpetual flux, utilizing the new information to shape his strategies and actions.

Jörmungandr

Jörmungandr, the Midgard Serpent, is an enigmatic figure of both terror and fascination in Norse mythology. Born to Loki and the giantess Angrboda, Jörmungandr serves as a mesmerizing symbol of the forces that both encircle and define the boundaries between the known and the unknown.

Its body stretches so extensively around the realm of Midgard that it can bite its own tail, creating an ouroboros—a perfect circle that encompasses the world itself. This self-engulfing act is not mere spectacle. On one hand, it underscores the interconnected fabric of life within Midgard, encapsulating the realm in a self-contained cycle. On the other hand, it echoes the very cycles of time and existence—an endless dance between creation and destruction. Although Jörmungandr may be perceived as menacing—especially given its foretold role during Ragnarök—its continuous encircling also acts as a linchpin that holds the very world together.

Regarding its relationship with Thor, the two are more than mere enemies; they are cosmic adversaries, representing the age-old tussle between order, embodied by Thor, and chaos, represented by Jörmungandr. Their conflicts, often manifesting as Thor's ill-fated fishing expeditions aimed at capturing the serpent, are not just squabbles but rather grand cosmic events. While Thor aims to bring order and safeguard Midgard, Jörmungandr exemplifies the aspects of existence that defy easy taming. And therein lies a delicate balance; neither can claim ultimate victory without disturbing the equilibrium that governs the cosmos.

As for Jörmungandr's character, unlike Thor, whose actions are often straightforward and direct, the serpent is elusive and cunning. It retreats into the depths of the ocean, emerging only when least expected, embodying traits that defy easy classification. Yes, it challenges the gods, but it also maintains a necessary tension that upholds the world's structure.

As Ragnarök approaches, Jörmungandr takes on a role of unparalleled significance. Emerging from the depths, it poisons the sky and engages in a cataclysmic showdown with Thor.

Fenrir

Fenrir, a wolf like no other, looms large in Norse mythology as a representation of untamed power and the inevitable course of destiny. Born to the trickster Loki and the giantess Angrboda, Fenrir's essence is a study in contradictions: he embodies elements that both demand our awe and stir our deepest fears. In his dual nature, we glimpse the complexities of destructive forces within the very fabric of the cosmos.

The gods observe Fenrir's growth, which is almost alarming in its rapidity, and are well aware of the dark prophecy that the wolf is destined to play a decisive role in Ragnarök. Efforts are made to contain this explosive force; yet Fenrir's formidable combination of strength and wit eludes their tactics. Eventually, it takes Gleipnir, a magical ribbon fashioned with subterfuge and artifice, to bind him. This extraordinary moment underscores not only Fenrir's cunning but also his indomitable spirit, compelling even the gods to resort to deception to rein him in.

The gods' actions are not propelled by malevolence but rather by a cocktail of emotions: fear, reverence, and a desperation to alter a destiny that remains largely outside their control. And here lies the irony—the very act of trying to ward off a terrible future fuels its manifestation. Fenrir, even when chained, seethes with growing fury and an unquenchable desire for freedom. His inevitable escape during Ragnarök is as much an outcome of the gods' intervention as it is a part of his intrinsic nature.

In Fenrir, we find a character who is neither purely villainous nor unequivocally noble. He embodies might and intelligence, and occupies a perplexing space as both a victim and a potent force of destiny.

Hel

Hel, the intriguing deity presiding over the Norse underworld, is the daughter of Loki and the giantess Angrboda. She is a sister to two equally complex figures: Fenrir and Jörmungandr. In Hel, we see encapsulated the very paradox of death—it is both an inescapable reality and an object of our primal fears. She is the ultimate arbiter of what comes after life, presiding over a realm that is transformative and final, yet also mysterious and shadowy.

Half alive and half skeletal—what an astonishing image that tells us so much about the nature of her domain! While you may think you know the underworld from other mythologies, which often feature fiery pits and eternal torments, Helheim is different. It defies such simple, hellish stereotypes. This is a place of eternal twilight, mirroring Hel's own dual nature. The realm she governs is neither a place of punitive suffering nor an eternal feast; it is rather a space of quiet, an everlasting pause that offers a respite from life's constant turmoil.

What's most fascinating is that Hel herself is a figure of great ambiguity. She is not a goddess who takes joy in the death of mortals and gods alike, yet she doesn't shun her role either. She embodies the inescapable gravity of mortality, a force even the gods must reckon with. They have a complex relationship with Hel, respecting her domain while also seeking to escape her grasp whenever possible. The tension is palpable: on one side is the intoxicating allure of life, and on the other, the inevitable finality that is death.

And how can we overlook the poignant episode of Baldr's demise? When the universally beloved god met his end, Hel set forth a simple yet impossible condition for his resurrection: everything in the cosmos must weep for him. As it turned out, not everything did. Hel, ever steadfast, upheld her decree. This reveals her as a deity of consistency and principle, who will not waver, even when faced with the most heart-wrenching of circumstances.

Einherjar

The Einherjar, elite warriors, represent a vivid manifestation of bravery and martial skill, elements deeply resonant in ancient Norse culture. The Einherjar serve a dual role in the grand scheme of things. On one hand, they symbolize the ultimate reward for valor in battle; on the other, they fulfill a more solemn function as a celestial army preparing for Ragnarök.

When a warrior falls heroically in battle, a Valkyrie immediately swoops down to escort his soul to Valhalla. In this otherworldly realm, Valkyries serve the warriors mead as they feast at the magnificent table of Odin himself. The atmosphere stands in dramatic contrast to that of Helheim, which offers an existence of eternal twilight and pause. Valhalla, by contrast, teems with energetic activities. Day after day, these chosen souls engage in battle, their wounds miraculously healing as each day concludes. The feast that follows each nightly battle serves as more than a celebration; it represents eternal renewal.

Valhalla's atmosphere is one of camaraderie, brotherhood, and mutual respect. After all, each Einherji has earned his seat in this heavenly realm through great deeds. The Norse sagas portray them as well-rounded human beings who possess not only physical prowess but also intellectual abilities—a warrior who can strategize, appreciates music, and has a penchant for poetry.

Yet, Valhalla also functions as a school for warriors, a place where the Einherjar prepare for Ragnarök. They are destined to join Odin and other gods in the ultimate showdown against the cosmic forces of chaos. Thus, they serve a purpose beyond simply receiving Odin's magnanimity; they play an instrumental role in determining the fate of the entire cosmos.

This multifaceted role elevates the Einherjar to figures of immense significance. They are not merely epitomes of bravery or martial skill; they embody a concept of heroism that transcends individual glory to include a sense of duty toward both the human community and the cosmos at large. This is not merely a mythic ideal. The legend of the Einherjar also acts as a potent motivating force in the earthly realm. It instills in warriors the aspiration to be brave, skilled, and honorable, offering them the ultimate reward of a seat in Valhalla.

Draugr

The Draugr, undead beings, personify a disturbing reversal of the natural order of things. Unlike the Einherjar or the peaceful souls in Helheim, the Draugr serve as a cautionary tale.

They embody anxieties about improper burials, unfulfilled lives, and the haunting notion that malevolence can persist even after death. Their physical form is often described as grotesque, swollen, and discolored—a frightening spectacle. These reanimated corpses are more than just physically menacing; they have an arsenal of magical abilities at their disposal. Some can manipulate the weather, others can change their shape, and some even have the uncanny ability to foresee the future. However, these powers are seldom used for virtuous deeds. Instead, Draugr are driven by a malevolent envy of the living and a desire to harm anyone who ventures near them. A chilling atmosphere often surrounds their burial mounds, marked by unsettling mist or unnaturally cold winds. Animals avoid these areas, sensing the dark aura that permeates them. These mounds are the dwelling places of the Draugr, who act as guardians of their own burial treasures—akin, in some ways, to dragons in other mythologies. These beings are not mindless monsters; they exhibit an eerie intelligence. Draugr can speak and even set traps, making them not only physical threats but also practitioners of psychological warfare. The sheer horror of encountering a being that exudes malevolence while possessing the cognitive ability to plan and strategize its evil intents is unimaginable.

Dealing with a Draugr is no straightforward task. A mere sword won't suffice.

One needs to engage both physically and spiritually with the creature, often aiming for the head with a ritualistic weapon and sometimes wrestling it back into its grave. After decapitating it, burning the remains is essential, and scattering the ashes into the sea ensures that the Draugr will never return.

Beyond their terrifying presence, Draugr carry deeper societal meaning. They symbolize the unease surrounding unfulfilled social and spiritual obligations. They serve as a grim reminder of the dire consequences of greed and the ever-present human capacity for envy and malevolence—traits that may not necessarily disappear with the end of life.

Dwarfs

Let us delve deep into the mythical caverns of Nidavellir, also known as Svartalfheim, where we meet the enigmatic Dwarfs, master artisans of the Norse world. This realm is a place of paradoxes: shadowy recesses filled with glowing gems and luminous ores. These caverns serve as the stage where Dwarfs, with their unique blend of earthiness and divinity, craft celestial objects of unimaginable potency. Don't be fooled by their small stature. These beings possess intrinsic might and an innate connection to earthly elements. In their forges, amid flickering flames and molten metal, they craft not just sturdy items but also magical artifacts. They grant divine beings tools and weapons that shape destiny. The marvels they create are imbued with enchantments that transform them from mere material objects into conduits of cosmic power. Yet these Dwarfs are more than skilled craftspeople. They are repositories of esoteric wisdom, often sought after by gods and heroes alike. However, one doesn't simply waltz into a Dwarf's abode and expect easy access to their guarded secrets. Gaining their wisdom often requires solving riddles or undergoing trials of wit, for these beings don't part with their knowledge lightly. The spectrum of their wisdom extends beyond crafting; they understand magical principles, the labyrinthine mechanics of the cosmos, and even the roots of the World Tree, Yggdrasil. This image of wisdom and craftsmanship shouldn't give you an impression of pure benevolence. Dwarfs have their own agendas, often motivated by keen interest in material gain. Think of them as shrewd traders who know the value of what they possess, driving hard bargains when gods or mortals come calling. This brings us to a somewhat unsettling facet: myths sometimes attribute darker traits to them, linking them to treacheries, curses, and unsettling manipulations of destiny itself. Consider the tale of the mead of poetry, a divine elixir that these Dwarfs once transformed into a catalyst for strife. Their complexity is fascinating. Just as the metals they manipulate can be molded into life-giving amulets or deadly weapons, so too do the Dwarfs embody a delicate balance between creation and destruction. They are pivotal figures in Norse cosmology, serving dual roles as both maintainers of cosmic order and instigators challenging the gods to face their own limitations and desires.

Elves

In a place where luminosity and grandeur dance in harmonious splendor, Alfheim stands as a realm so ethereal that it is said to be beyond mortal comprehension. The influence of Elves reaches into the worlds of gods and humans alike.

When you think of Elves, picture beings who radiate qualities of light: purity, wisdom, and a form of spiritual elevation that seems to rise above the material world. Often referred to as "Light Elves," they stand in stark contrast to Dwarfs, who are sometimes called "Dark Elves" and whose essence is deeply tied to earthly matter. Elves serve as ethereal counterpoints, more aligned with realms of magic, foresight, and healing arts—pursuits that echo their luminous nature.

Their appearance is so fair and radiant that it would awe or perhaps even intimidate both gods and mortals. While their physical beauty is remarkable, it acts as a visual echo or metaphor for their true nature, which is oriented toward loftier planes of wisdom and spirituality. In a sense, their appearance serves as an external manifestation of their internal richness.

Although they are not gods, Elves are often seen as kin or allies to the divine, especially the Vanir gods, with whom they share mutual interests in fertility and prosperity. Their realm is tranquil, yet they do not shy away from participating in divine events and even cosmic conflicts, blending elements of peace and dynamism into their existence.

Surprisingly, despite their otherworldly attributes, Elves are not aloof entities removed from the concerns of mortals. Folklore and sagas abound with stories of their interactions with humans. Elves possess the ability to shape-shift or turn invisible, navigating between realms to guide, challenge, or sometimes complicate human lives. Whether through blessings, magical artifacts, or even the affliction of illnesses, their actions are dictated by a complex moral code.

Moreover, there is an ecological dimension to their existence. Elves serve as mythical custodians of natural beauty, acting as guardians of forests, lakes, and wild places. They stand as symbols of the awe and respect that the natural world should inspire in us, serving as both a moral and environmental compass guiding our interactions with nature.

Hulder (Huldra)

The Hulder is a figure who perfectly embodies the untamed duality of nature itself. She appears as a woman of breathtaking beauty deep within a forest or beside a shimmering body of water. But don't judge too quickly by appearances; her back might reveal the hollow of a tree or even a cow's tail. This fascinating duality serves as a metaphorical caution, urging us to look beyond what meets the eye.

The settings where the Hulder typically resides—forests, lakes—are places that evoke an innate wildness. Here, her haunting melodies echo, luring the curious or the lost. Her intentions defy easy categorization. Some stories depict her as a benevolent force, guiding lost souls home or bestowing wisdom upon them. Yet in other tales, she morphs into a predatory entity, leading men to their unfortunate fates.

Her relationship with the wilderness serves as more than just a backdrop for her stories; it's integral to her very essence. Consider her a guardian of animals, a shape-shifter, and a being deeply rooted in natural elements. Her influence extends beyond the forest; she also plays a role in agriculture. Winning her favor could result in the blessings of a bountiful harvest, while incurring her wrath might lead to dire consequences, such as crop failure.

Although she's not a goddess in the strict sense, the Hulder does possess qualities that border on the divine. She has the extraordinary ability to become invisible, to cast illusions, and even to reveal the secrets of hidden treasures. These are no minor abilities; yet, she also has earthly concerns. Many tales poignantly reveal her quest for a human soul, often sought through matrimonial bonds with human men. This aspect adds a layer of tragedy to her character, marking her as a creature forever balanced on the edge between two worlds.

What most captivates us about the Hulder is her ability to challenge our perceptions—of nature, of humanity, and of the lines dividing the cultivated from the untamed. She emerges from the cultural fabric as a reflection of our complex relationship with the natural world and serves as a mirror, urging us to confront our own intricacies and hidden dualities.

Kraken

The Kraken is a mythical creature that haunts the far reaches of the Northern European seas, particularly in Scandinavian folklore. This being is so immense that its body could easily be mistaken for an island. However, the Kraken is more than just a fantastical tale born from the imaginations of fishermen. It serves as a grand metaphor for humankind's primal fear of the unknown abyss—the enigmatic and boundless ocean that still defies full understanding.

Its tentacles are a feature that imprints itself in your memory. These appendages possess enough strength to pull entire ships, along with their hapless crews, down into the dark, watery abyss. To add a layer of intricacy and terror, these tentacles are often described as extraordinarily long, even extending well above the water's surface. As if this weren't enough to terrify, there are reports and artistic interpretations that embellish the creature with sharp beaks or even multiple heads, as though challenging us to stretch our imaginations to their very limits.

The Kraken symbolizes the ocean's inscrutable magnitude and complexity. Its appearance is often accompanied by phenomena like whirlpools and turbulent waves. This is not mere happenstance; it's an acknowledgment of the creature's seemingly elemental influence over its watery domain. The Kraken serves as a challenge to human bravado, reminding us that our mastery over nature has its limits.

The locale of this mythical creature is as evocative as its form. It resides in the remote depths of the ocean, far from the familiar coasts where human communities dwell. The Kraken seems to embody the distant mysteries and dangers of those uncharted waters, becoming a symbol for the ultimate unknown—a siren call that has both lured and deterred explorers throughout history. In an era when the limits of human understanding were far less expansive than they are today, the Kraken served as a powerful cautionary emblem, warning of the perils, even doom, that awaited those daring enough to stray too far from the known into the abyss of the great unknown.

Ratatoskr

Ratatoskr, a squirrel of extraordinary agility and quickness, perpetually darts up and down the trunk of the majestic Yggdrasil. He is far more than just a woodland creature in a fairytale setting. He serves as a unique messenger, shuttling messages between two cosmic beings: the dragon Níðhǫggr, which gnaws at the roots below, and the eagle perched on the topmost branches. This is not a postal service based on friendliness; rather, Ratatoskr specializes in provocations, taunts, and insults. In doing so, he does more than merely pass along information; he actively perpetuates cosmic tension that is integral to the Norse understanding of the universe.

Ratatoskr's route is not horizontal but rather vertical, running along the length of Yggdrasil. In this movement, he transcends boundaries, linking different realms and beings that would otherwise remain disconnected. This vertical axis serves as a potent symbol. Ratatoskr is at the crossroads, embodying the principle that everything is intertwined, from the roots to the heavens. Even minor exchanges can have repercussions that resonate across the cosmos. However, let's not forget: Ratatoskr's messaging service comes with risks, revealing that communication can distort as much as it can connect—it is hardly a straightforward instrument of harmony.

There's also an ecological perspective to consider. Yggdrasil itself represents the cosmos, and our agile squirrel symbolizes the ceaseless flow of energy and matter within a living ecosystem. He serves as a representation of the very essence of balance in nature, constantly in motion, but also serving as a cog in a much larger, finely tuned machine.

Trolls

Trolls—the quintessential outsiders in Norse stories—lurk under old stone bridges, hide in dark, enigmatic caves, or dwell in secluded mountain ranges and untouched forests.

When it comes to their appearances, trolls are marvelously varied. They can be enormous, almost mountain-like, or roughly the size of an average human. Sometimes they are depicted as grotesquely ugly; at other times, they are so stunningly attractive that they could pass for humans. Some narratives even attribute shape-shifting capabilities to trolls, enabling them to assume various forms to deceive or manipulate those who encounter them. This diverse range of physical characteristics serves as an external reflection of their complex relationship with the human world. Both unsettlingly strange and uncomfortably familiar, they captivate our imaginations while simultaneously arousing our most primitive fears.

Masters of deception, trolls scheme with riddles or employ brute force to lure humans into their hidden domains. And once you're caught? Well, the tales vary. They range from the grim prospect of being eaten to the sorrowful fate of lifelong enslavement. Yet it would be hasty to pigeonhole trolls as merely malevolent creatures. Some stories offer another dimension, portraying trolls as misunderstood, solitary beings who are susceptible to kindness and even capable of profound change. This moral duality makes trolls characters of enduring complexity and fascination.

Trolls are creatures of the night, avoiding daylight as though it were poison. Legends claim that exposure to sunlight can transform them into stone. This intriguing feature heightens their role as beings that dwell on boundaries—always oscillating between the light and the dark, and between the civilized world and the untamed wilderness.

They are also potent sorcerers. With abilities that range from cursing individuals to manipulating weather patterns, and even foretelling the future, trolls are elevated from mere brutes to formidable, supernatural entities.

Often linked to far-off, untamed lands, trolls are more than mere inhabitants of the natural world. They personify it, epitomizing both its alluring beauty and its lurking dangers. By existing in these remote locations, trolls also serve as living, breathing embodiments of the inherent risks and treasures found in nature.

Valkyries

The Valkyries, awe-inspiring warrior maidens, serve as a fascinating bridge between the realms of gods and men. Tasked by Odin with selecting fallen warriors from the battlegrounds and guiding them to Valhalla, their role is crucial in preparing for Ragnarök. These figures are of immense complexity, symbolizing valor, loyalty, and the intricate dance between fate and free will. They possess a beauty that combines an almost ethereal grace with the formidable strength of warriors. Clad in shining armor and carrying spears or swords, their allure presents a powerful contrast to the grim reality of their mission. This duality creates captivating tension between elements usually considered opposites: beauty and danger, life and death.

Far from being mere damsels, these women are warriors of exceptional strength and martial prowess. Despite this, they are not simply divine automata programmed to carry out Odin's wishes. Sagas and tales often portray them as individuals with their own desires, capable of defying even Odin himself. Characters like Brynhildr have chosen to disobey Odin for the sake of love or personal belief, adding an intriguing layer of nuance to our understanding of the tension between duty and choice.

Beyond guiding souls to Valhalla, Valkyries possess the power to influence mortal battles. They bestow their favor upon chosen warriors while denying it to others. Warriors in the heat of combat invoke their names, hoping against hope to be selected for glory rather than doom. A Valkyrie's appearance on the battlefield is therefore both a coveted blessing and a feared omen.

In Valhalla, they wait upon the chosen warriors—the Einherjar—who are themselves preparing for the cataclysmic events of Ragnarök. By serving in this hospitable manner, the Valkyries reveal another facet of their character. This domestic duty does not diminish their martial nature; on the contrary, it complements it, broadening our understanding of their intricate personalities.

Over the centuries, the figure of the Valkyrie has evolved, inspiring countless interpretations, particularly in modern popular culture. While these modern adaptations may seem anachronistic, they encapsulate the essence of these complex, powerful beings. Valkyries today are often viewed as epitomes of both physical and moral courage—strong, independent women who defy easy categorization.

Sleipnir

Sleipnir is a steed with eight legs, the favored horse of Odin himself. It serves as a repository for intricate themes such as transformation, duality, and the fascinating intersection between the divine and the natural world.

To understand Sleipnir, one must start with its lineage. Born to Loki, the god known for shape-shifting and cunning, and Svaðilfari, a stallion of near-mythical prowess, Sleipnir's parentage sets the stage for its exceptional qualities. This lineage unites the divine and the mortal, the chaotic and the sublime, synthesizing them into a creature that transcends both realms.

What immediately captivates our imagination is Sleipnir's extraordinary appearance. Encountering an eight-legged horse is not an everyday experience, neither in the realm of men nor among the gods in Asgard. These additional limbs are not mere ornamentation; they symbolize greater speed and power, elevating Sleipnir beyond any horse you have ever known. And then there is its color—gray, neither black nor white. This color signifies Sleipnir's role as a creature that exists between worlds, on the threshold of realities.

Speaking of thresholds, Sleipnir is no ordinary horse restricted to the confines of Asgard. It can traverse all Nine Worlds, embodying exceptional versatility and mobility. It serves as a bridge between realms, a creature that defies limitations and laughs in the face of geographical constraints.

Another point of interest is the extraordinary loyalty between Sleipnir and Odin. Their relationship is not one of subjugation but a mutual bond rooted in respect. Odin takes excellent care of Sleipnir, and the horse, in turn, serves Odin faithfully. This relationship stands as a reminder that bonds can indeed form based on mutual respect—even across different realms and species.

Mare

Ah, the Mares! These mystical creatures certainly know how to send a shiver down your spine. They were infamous for tormenting the dreams of their victims and causing some of the most terrifying nightmares one could imagine. The notion that they were living souls roaming freely, separate from their physical bodies, only intensified their creepiness. Moreover, they were believed to sit on people's shoulders while they slept, a detail sufficient to make anyone double-check their locks at night. Despite their frightening reputation, the Mares continue to be a fascinating part of Norse mythology, captivating the minds of enthusiasts everywhere.

CHAPTER 6
The Most Compelling and Fascinating Myths

Let us tell you all about the fascinating Norse myths. This is a rich tapestry of stories, beliefs, customs, and history woven by the Germanic-speaking peoples of Northern Europe. From the frosty lands of Denmark, Finland, Iceland, Sweden, and Norway, these myths and tales were passed down from generation to generation, capturing the imaginations and hearts of the pre-Christian Germanic people.

But as time passed and Christianity took hold, the once-thriving beliefs of the Norse people began to fade. However, their stories and legends have lived on and have captured the interest of people for centuries.

So if you're looking for a good story, a bit of tradition, or just a touch of magic, dive into the most compelling and fascinating myths. Trust us, you won't regret it!

The Creation Myth

In the beginning, there was a vast void called Ginnungagap, which lay between the realm of fire, Muspellheimr, and Niflheimr, the frozen land of mists. This void was completely devoid of life and any form of matter.

One day, the cold mists of Niflheimr began to spread through Ginnungagap, forming a great block of ice. As the temperature of Muspellheimr rose, the heat from the fire began to melt the block of ice, and from it emerged Ymir, a primeval deity who had been hibernating.

Although still asleep, Ymir sweated from the heat of Muspellheimr, and from his sweat the first living creatures were born. In addition, a great cow called Audhumla emerged from the ice, and her udders became the source of the four rivers that fed Ymir.

The cow fed by licking a salty block of ice, and as she did so a new creature was born. This creature is Buri, the progenitor of the gods. Meanwhile, Ymir continued to create life, giving rise to the Jotun, the giants.

Buri mated with a giant to give birth to Borr, who mated with the giantess Bestla to give birth to Odin, Vili and Ve. After that, Odin, Vili and Ve were frustrated and bored in the void of Ginnungagap because there was still no sky, earth, sea, or forests. The brothers decided that it was time to do something and that only the death of Ymir would usher in the world we know today. Odin, Vili and Ve attacked and killed the giant Ymir and created the world we know today.

From Ymir's blood came the oceans, from his flesh came the land, and his great bones were piled up to form mountain ranges. In Ymir's flesh were small larvae that became dwarves who would live underground and noble elves who would populate Alfheimr.

After shaping Midgard, the gods realized that it could not be uninhabited. They saw two trunks at the edge of the ocean and decided to use this material to create mankind. A man called Askr and a woman called Embla were created. Odin gave them life, Vili gave them intelligence, and Ve sculpted their eyes, ears, and mouth so they could hear, see, and speak.

All humans are descended from this first couple, and Odin is known as the Supreme Father.

Eventually the brothers created the realm of Asgard, the home of the gods, which was separate from the other realms and connected only by the Bifrost Bridge. This was the beginning of the Gods' rule over the world.

Odin's eye

After creating the world over the body of the giant Ymir, who was killed by the gods, the wise and powerful Odin continued to rule from his throne in Asgard. Despite his vast knowledge, Odin knew that there was always more to learn. So he embarked on a daring adventure in search of the secrets of the universe.

To gain the knowledge he sought, Odin had to travel through Jotunheimr, the land of giants and enemies of the gods. Disguised as a humble wanderer, he made his way to the residence of his uncle, Mimir. Mimir was a very old and wise deity who lived near the Well of Knowledge, the source of the life-giving waters that fed Yggdrasill, the Tree of World.

Odin approached his uncle and humbly asked to drink from the well. But Mimir was not easily persuaded by his nephew's elevated position. He knew the true cost of the knowledge found in the well and demanded a high price.

"The price of the water of knowledge is high, grandson," Mimir said. "Higher than you can imagine. It requires sacrifice."

Willing to pay any price for true wisdom, Odin asked his uncle what he should do.

"The price is your eye," Mimir said. "Tear it out and throw it in the well; only then can you drink from it."

Odin knew his uncle was not joking. The sacrifice he demanded was a great one, but the god did not hesitate. With a scream of pain that echoed throughout the universe, Odin tore out his eye and threw it into the well.

Mimir was pleased with Odin's sacrifice and gave the one-eyed man a horn of the well's water. Odin drank deeply, consuming the entire contents of the vessel at once. And so he was filled with the knowledge he sought.

Though he had lost an eye, Odin's sacrifice had given him greater vision and insight than ever before. He could see the world more clearly than ever before, and the great scar that filled the void where his eye used to be would sometimes emit a bright flame, distinguishing him as the one-eyed man or the one with the flaming eye. So Odin returned to his throne in Asgard, wiser and more powerful than ever, with the knowledge he had sought and the sacrifice he had made forever imprinted upon him.

Loki and the Gifts of the Gods - Origin of Thor's Hammer

The goddess Sif, wife of the mighty Thor, was famous for her beautiful and long golden hair. The god of thunder admired and adored this feature of hers. One day, however, Thor returned to Asgard and was confronted with a shocking scene: Sif had been stripped of her hair during the night, thanks to a trick played by the god of deception, Loki.

Thor, already furious after an unsuccessful fishing expedition against Jormungandr, dragged Loki into his room, where Sif was crying desperately. In an angry tone, Thor exclaimed, "Look what you have done! You cut off my wife's hair! Now I have to walk around with a bald woman at my side?"

Loki, trying to save himself, suggested, "Have you ever thought of having her wear a hat?" This suggestion did not appease Thor, who threatened, "If you do not find a way to restore the luster to Sif's hair, I will break every bone in your body!"

With this threat, Loki set out to find a solution. He traveled to Nidavellir, the land of the dwarves, confident that their skilled craftsmen could build anything. Before asking for their help, he decided to challenge them. He turned to the sons of Ívaldi, known for their craftsmanship, and said, "Have you heard the latest news? The gods are holding a competition to see who is the best craftsman, and the brothers Brokkr and Eitri have told you, the sons of Ívaldi i, that you don't stand a chance."

The sons of Ívaldi were offended by Loki's words and retorted, "This is an insult! The calloused hands of these brothers will not stand a chance against us! Satisfied with their response, Loki proposed a deal: "Very well. But there's one condition. You must build three gifts for the gods, and one of them must be long, golden hair that never stops growing.

Loki, always looking for new ways to create chaos, decided to encourage the brothers Brokkr and Eitri to enter the Gods' contest. "You won't believe this, but the sons of Ívaldi are competing to see who is the best craftsman," he told them. "And they have said that you, brothers, don't stand a chance because you are just bunglers."

Brokkr and Eitri, offended by Loki's words, replied, "That is typical of the sons of Ívaldi. Everyone knows that we are far more skilled than they are. We have nothing to gain from this competition.

Loki, determined to challenge them, proposed a wager: "I wager that you are no better than the legendary Sons of Ívaldi. I wager my own head."

Brokkr, ready to accept the challenge, said, "The head of the most elusive of gods is too tempting a prize not to accept. We are ready to wager."

Loki swallowed hard, but accepted the wager. He knew that Brokkr and Eitri were very skilled, but now he would have to use all his cunning to prevent them from winning. The dwarves and the sons of Ívaldi began to prepare their gifts for the gods, and Loki noticed that everything seemed to go well.

But when he saw that the brothers Brokkr and Eitri were creating an

extraordinary piece, a powerful hammer, he realized that he had to intervene. To achieve perfection, the dwarves had to keep the forge at the ideal temperature, not one degree more or less. And Brokkr did his job with precision, pumping the bellows.
Loki, determined to prevent him from completing his task, transformed into a blood-sucking mosquito and flew toward Brokkr. First he stung him painfully on the hand, then on the neck, but the dwarf endured the pain and continued working. Finally, Loki decided to attack the dwarf's eyes, but he closed them and allowed himself to be stung on the eyelids. The agony was unbearable, and the dwarf stopped pumping the bellows. The handle of the hammer broke due to the temperature fluctuations.
Loki considered his mission accomplished and left, leaving the brothers Brokkr and Eitri to tend to their wounds.
The contest was finally over, and the dwarves—the sons of Ívaldi, presented their gifts to the gods. Sif, the beautiful wife of Thor, was given new, very long golden hair that made her look even more enchanting than before. Loki, though relieved, knew he still had to save himself from the bet he had lost.
Odin was given an extraordinary spear called Gungnir, which could pierce anything, and any oath made under it would be unbreakable. Freyr, the god of wealth, was given a huge boat called Skidbladnir that could sail anywhere and could be folded so many times that it could fit in a pocket.
Brokkr and Eitri, no less, presented their gifts. Odin received a ring of pure gold, called Draupnir, which produced eight identical copies of equal value every nine nights. Freyr was given a magnificent boar with a golden coat, called Gullinbursti, which could fly without tiring and whose splendor chased away the darkness.
Finally, it was Thor's turn. He was presented with a hammer, Mjolnir, which at first seemed to have a handle that was too short. But Brokkr explained that the hammer should not be judged by its handle, for Mjolnir was indestructible and its power almost indescribable. When thrown, it never missed its mark and always returned to its owner.
Thor exclaimed, "What a wonderful piece! With this powerful hammer, no giant will be my equal!" Odin and Freyr also agreed that, of all the gifts, the hammer Mjolnir was definitely the best.
Loki, who had lost the wager, now had to face the consequences. Brokkr, already sharpening his axe, said, "Now I want your head. But Loki had one last card to play.
Loki: "You can cut off my head, as long as you don't damage any part of my neck. The deal says you can only have my head."
Brokkr: "You cheat; how can I take your head without damaging the neck?"
Odin intervened and said, "If people paid more attention to the words they used, they would never negotiate with the cunning trickster Loki."
Brokkr then decided to punish Loki by sewing his mouth shut so that he would

not be able to deceive anyone for a long time. But at least the deceiver kept his head on his shoulders, and the gods of Asgard received magnificent artifacts.

The Day that Loki became a Mother

Asgard was the home of the greatest gods of Norse mythology, known as the Aesir. These powerful gods had many enemies from many different lineages, but they all feared Thor, the champion of the gods.

With his mighty hammer Mjolnir, Thor was able to protect the stronghold of the gods, but he also had an adventurous spirit, always seeking new challenges. He couldn't stay still and was constantly on the move, exploring new lands and encountering new enemies. In his absence, Asgard was vulnerable to its enemies. To protect Asgard, the gods decided to build a very high and thick wall, but they knew it would take years to complete.

One day, a muscular traveler came to Asgard, claiming to be a great builder who could build the wall in a year. In return, he asked for the hand of the beautiful goddess Freyja. The gods rejected his proposal, believing it to be outrageous.

But the cunning Loki suggested that they accept the builder's proposal and set him a deadline. "Hear me, my friends," said Loki. "If we accept his proposal, the builder will never finish the wall in a year, and he will get nothing. But if we let him work, he will still have built a good part of the wall, and we will save ourselves a great deal of trouble".

The gods agreed to Loki's proposal and accepted the contract with the builder. The builder set to work with great haste, and the wall quickly took shape. However, the gods realized that the deadline was very close and that the builder had almost finished the work.

Odin became furious with Loki, blaming him for what had happened: "The wall is almost finished. We will surely lose our beloved Freyja to this man. And it's all your fault!"

Loki realized that the builder would not be able to complete the task without the help of the mighty stallion. So he devised a plan to keep the horse away from the site.

Loki transformed himself into a beautiful mare and attracted the attention of the master builder's mighty horse. The horse was blinded by the god in disguise, and the builder was unable to control the horse's impulse to run after the divine mare. Running as fast as he could, Loki disappeared over the horizon with the stallion in his wake.

Without the help of his horse, the builder was unable to finish the job in time and turned on the gods, revealing his true identity: he was a giant. "Damn the gods of Asgard! You are nothing but tricksters! You will meet your end!" the angry giant shouted.

The giant began to attack the gods, but Thor, the champion of the gods, confronted him and struck him down with his mighty hammer, Mjolnir, smashing his head in.

The gods of Asgard completed the rest of the wall, and at last the Aesir homeland was safe. But much time passed before Loki returned to Asgard. The gods worried about him, fearing that he was in danger.

After a long time, Loki finally returned, bringing with him an exotic and extraordinary eight-legged foal that followed him wherever he went. Loki offered the foal to Odin, assuring him that when it grew up, it would be the fastest and most powerful horse ever.

But there was one condition: no one could ever ask him about the origin of this majestic horse. Odin looked at Loki suspiciously but accepted the gift. The exotic colt would be known as Sleipnir.

Thor's Hammer Theft

Thor, the mighty god of thunder, was equipped with the powerful hammer Mjolnir, given to him by the dwarves after a prank by the god Loki. With this hammer, Thor defended the realm of Asgard against all threats.

One day, however, Thor awoke to find that his beloved hammer was missing. With a mixture of concern and determination, Thor searched his room for Mjolnir, only to find a message that read, "If you want your hammer back, come to me in my territories. We can negotiate a fair ransom. Signed: Thrim".

Thor knew that the best person to negotiate with Thrim was none other than Loki, the god of mischief. And so Thor asked Loki to go in his place to meet Thrim in the land of the giants.

Loki arrived in Jotunheimr and presented himself to Thrim. When the giant saw him, he immediately noticed the difference between him and Thor and said: "Dear Thor, come closer, for my sight is not as good as it once was. You are thinner than when we last met".

Loki, clever as he was, immediately realized the giant's weakness and began to negotiate. After the negotiations, he returned to Asgard with Thrim's proposal: the giant was willing to return the hammer if Freyja, the most beautiful of the goddesses, was given to him as a wife.

The gods found the proposal outrageous and decided not to accept it. But without Mjolnir, Thor could not defend Asgard. And it was then that Loki had a truly extraordinary idea.

Loki said to Thor: "You must wear this!" And he showed him a wedding dress. Thor, of course, was shocked and said: "How dare you insult me like that?" But Loki replied: "Calm down; I'll explain my plan later".

Loki knew that Thrim's eyesight was not very good and that he wouldn't be able to recognize Thor dressed as a woman. And so, for want of a better alternative, Thor decided to disguise himself as a bride and follow Loki, who was also dressed as Freyja's servant.

When they arrived in Jotunheimr, they were greeted with great honor by Thrim, who had organized a banquet in honor of the beautiful goddess. The giant, of course, did not realize that the "goddess Freyja" was actually Thor in disguise, and this gave Loki the opportunity to put his plan into action.

During the banquet, Thrim noticed Thor's voracious appetite and said: "Wow, what a voracious appetite you have, my new wife. I have never seen a goddess as ravenous as you.

At this point Loki intervened and said: "I think she wants the feast to end as soon as possible so you can consummate your union." Thor gave a dirty look to Loki, who seemed to find the whole situation very funny.

Thrim, unaware of Thor's true identity, said: "So be it; bring the hammer. We will seal the deal and settle this." One of the giant's servants brought the hammer and placed it before the bride.

Thor, finally free to unleash his fury, grabbed the hammer and crushed all of the giant's servants with one blow. Thrim, overwhelmed by Thor's fury, could not resist and was killed.

With the hammer finally recovered and the giant's threat defeated, Thor couldn't wait to go home and take off the hideous wedding dress. But Loki, with his mischievous spirit, reminded him that a good widow must wear black.

The kingdom of Asgard was safe again, thanks to Thor's heroism and Loki's cunning. And the gods never stopped having fun at the banquets of Valhalla, telling the story of how Thor disguised himself as a bride to retrieve his hammer.

Loki's Children

Loki, the god of mischief in Norse mythology, was the protagonist of many surprising and entertaining adventures, but he also had a malicious side that led to the downfall of the Aesir.

Loki had a faithful wife, Sigyn, with whom he had two sons, Narfi and Vali. Another famous son of Loki was Sleipnir, Odin's eight-legged horse, who was conceived in a very bizarre affair.

But the most incredible story concerns the heart of a beautiful giantess named Angrboda. One day, Loki found the roasted heart among the ashes and decided to eat it. As a result, he became pregnant and gave birth to a dangerous offspring.

Odin, the ruler of Asgard, had a vision in which he saw a great battle between the Asgardians and the forces of darkness. These children played a very important role in this conflict, and his last vision was the jaws of a giant wolf, after which his vision became completely blurred. Odin was very concerned and forced Loki to reveal the whereabouts of his children. The gods then went to Jotunheimr in search of Loki's children. When the gods found them, they found that the children were very young. One of them was a serpent, another was a wolf cub, and the third was a beautiful girl, but when she turned her face, the gods saw that the other side of her body had the appearance of a decaying corpse. This girl was named Hel and had a very frightening appearance.

The gods took the children and brought them to Asgard, but the return journey took some time. During the journey, Odin noticed that the serpent had doubled in size and realized that it would become extremely dangerous. So he decided to throw it into the great sea that surrounded Midgard. The snake grew so large over time that it encircled the world and reached its tail. This snake became known as Jörmungandr and became a very important figure in Norse mythology.

Hel was regarded with suspicion and fear by the other gods. Odin, noticing that she preferred the company of the dead to that of the living, decided to make her ruler of the world of the dead, where she would rule over the souls of those who had died in an unworthy manner and had not reached Valhalla.

The wolf cub, on the other hand, grew up among the gods of Asgard and learned their language. His name was Fenrir, and he became a friend of Tyr, who formed a very strong bond with him. However, like Jörmungandr the serpent, Fenrir continued to grow rapidly, becoming larger than a bull and soon bigger than any animal on earth.

Unfortunately, Fenrir also inherited some of the worst traits of his father, Loki, including malice and cruelty. The gods realized they had to do something to neutralize this threat. After much discussion, they decided to devise a plan to keep the overgrown wolf in check.

Fenrir's imprisonment

The mighty wolf Fenrir continued to grow, and the gods of Asgard became very concerned. All the gods looked at the beast with suspicion, except for the god Tyr, who had a bond of friendship with the wolf. The gods of Asgard decided to create powerful chains to keep Fenrir captive, but to hide their intentions, they proposed a challenge.

Fenrir loved a challenge and agreed to free himself from the chains the gods had constructed. The gods chained the giant beast, but the strong chains were useless against his strength. A new, even stronger chain was created, but it too was destroyed by the wolf's strength.

The gods were stunned by the sheer power of the wolf, and Fenrir sensed their fear, a sign that they were plotting something. Odin knew that only the dwarves could create a chain capable of containing the power of Fenrir.

Odin ordered the elf Skírnir to go to the land of the Dwarves and ask them to create something that could contain the wolf. The dwarves agreed and provided a list of strange ingredients to be used: roots from a mountain, a bear's sinew, a woman's beard, fish breath, bird saliva, and finally the sound of a cat's footsteps. After gathering all the ingredients, the dwarves went to work and created a rope called Gleipnir, which appeared to be made of silk.

Fenrir was once again asked to break these bonds, but he was already suspicious. When he saw the rope, he suspected treachery on the part of the gods. Odin tried to reassure the wolf that it was just for fun, but the wolf didn't get along with Odin, and as Loki's son, he could smell the lie on Odin's breath.

The wolf offered a challenge. He would only participate in the joke if a god dared to put his hand in his mouth while the animal was being held. If there was treachery, he would devour the hand without hesitation. The gods looked at each other, confirming the wolf's suspicion.

Tyr, the god who had always nurtured Fenrir and who had formed a bond of friendship with the beast, decided to put his hand in the wolf's mouth to help the other gods keep him captive. Fenrir agreed to be bound once more by the gods. He fought the bonds with all his might but could not break them, thanks to the skill of the dwarves who had made them. Seeing the satisfaction in the eyes of the gods, except for Tyr, who seemed sorry, Fenrir realized that he had been betrayed by both the gods and his only friend. With one last burst of rage, the wolf clenched his jaws and ripped Tyr's hand from his body. The brave god bore the pain in silence, becoming a hero for his sacrifice. The gods of Asgard were finally relieved, for they had neutralized the threat of Fenrir.

Finally, the wolf roared in anger, insulting the gods and declaring that he could have been their friend. But now, because of their treachery, they had become his greatest enemies. Fenrir swore revenge against Odin on the battlefield during Ragnarök.

Baldr's sad end

Baldr was the beloved son of Odin and Frigga, the rulers of Asgard. He was a very handsome and charming god, with a charisma that made him loved by all. His presence brought joy and happiness wherever he went. At night, however, this happiness disappeared, and his sleep was plagued by dark and disturbing nightmares. His beloved wife Nanna comforted him each time he woke in terror, but none of the gods knew the meaning of these dreams.

The wise Odin knew that there was an oracle in the realm of Hel, the place where the souls of the dead who did not die an honorable death on the battlefield went to rest. This oracle could decipher the nightmares that plagued Baldr. So Odin disguised himself as a vagabond and ventured into the realm of the dead to discover what was tormenting his son.

After consulting the runes, the oracle answered Odin with a sad message: "Helehimr is preparing to receive Baldr. When pain strikes Asgard, the realm of the dead will be illuminated by the joy of the arrival of the gentle spirit of Baldr." With a heavy heart, Odin returned to Asgard to share the prophecy with Frigga. Frigga was determined to prevent her son's fate. She knew that Baldr was loved by all, so she asked all the gods and creatures to swear never to harm Baldr. Even weapons, plants, diseases, and all objects swore not to harm the god.

Loki, the god of deception, who had chaos in his nature, was not particularly happy with this oath but was forced to take it like all the others. And so Baldr became invulnerable to everything and safe from all danger. Peace and serenity returned to Asgard, knowing that their beloved Baldr was safe.

Baldr's invulnerability brought joy to the gods, who challenged him by throwing objects at him, but all were deflected. Even Thor tried to hit him with his mighty hammer, but Baldr felt nothing, and everyone in Asgard was happy to know that their beloved god was protected. The only one who was not satisfied was Loki, who was determined to find his weakness.

One day, Loki secretly overheard a conversation between Frigga and a friend in which the goddess mentioned that she had made all things swear not to harm

Baldr, except for mistletoe, a harmless plant. But in Loki's mischievous mind, mistletoe was not so harmless. After gathering some mistletoe, he turned to the gods, who were still having fun trying to hit Baldr. Only the blind god Hodr was sad to be excluded from the game, for he could not participate without knowing where Baldr was.

The clever Loki made a dart out of mistletoe. He then approached Hodr, the blind god, and told him not to let his blindness keep him from participating in the game. Loki became invisible and led Hodr to the other gods. Baldr, happy to see Hodr in the game, welcomed the throw with enthusiasm.

With Loki's help, Hodr threw the dart with all his might and hit Baldr. Hodr expected to hear the laughter of the gods, but instead, a deep silence fell over the scene. Baldr was mortally wounded, and his lifeless body lay on the ground. The gods wept in despair at his death, and as prophesied, the world of the living was struck with grief at the loss of their beloved Baldr. His death marked the beginning of a long series of events that would forever change the fate of Asgard and its inhabitants.

The time when Thor tried to capture Jörmungandr

Asgard's gods traveled to the famous palace of Ægir, the sea god revered by sailors. Legend has it that the feasts Ægir hosted were extraordinary and that an unforgettable mead was served. However, when the gods arrived, Ægir pretended to be unable to host a great feast because he did not have a cauldron large enough to make the mead they wanted.

Tyr, the god of war, was aware that his father Hymir possessed a massive cauldron that would be ideal for Ægir's requirements. Together with Thor, they decided to search for Hymir. When they arrived, they were greeted by Tyr's mother, who suggested that the only way to get the cauldron was to appease Hymir.

Hymir invited the gods to a feast, and Thor, famous for his insatiable hunger, did not disappoint, devouring an entire ox. Impressed by Thor's appetite, Hymir declared that he would go fishing for whales to feed the guests.

Thor was eager to go fishing with Hymir the Giant, but Hymir was skeptical of Thor's ability to handle the open sea. Nevertheless, the god of thunder felt challenged and declared himself a better fisherman than anyone else.

So the two set sail in search of a legendary prey. It didn't take Hymir long to catch something big, but Thor was determined to do better by rowing into even deeper waters. Despite Hymir's warning about the territory of the World Serpent, Jörmungandr, Thor decided to try to catch something even bigger, using a bull's head as bait. His skill and determination were soon rewarded when he felt something huge bite. The boat began to be pulled with great force, and suddenly the giant serpent emerged from the depths. Thor had succeeded in capturing Jörmungandr!

The fight between Thor and Jörmungandr was intense, and Hymir was desperate, fearing that they would be dragged to the bottom of the ocean.

However, Thor had already faced the monstrous serpent in the past and vowed to take his revenge.

As the battle continued, Thor desperately tried to pull the serpent within reach of his hammer. Just as it seemed that Thor was about to gain the upper hand, Hymir cut the fishing line, allowing Jörmungandr to escape at the last moment. Thor was furious, so much so that he wanted to split Hymir's head open, if only he weren't Tyr's father.

The gods left with the cauldron, which would be necessary for making mead for Ægir's party, after filling their stomachs with whale meat. While all the gods were enjoying themselves, Thor could not forget Jörmungandr and vowed to kill the dark creature in the future. And so it was that Thor and Jörmungandr were destined to meet again during Ragnarök.

The Punishment of Loki

Loki had a great propensity for chaos; he was a bringer of discord and a destroyer of harmony, and this led him to devise a plan to kill Baldr. The gods, worried about Baldr's fate, decided to send Hermodr, the messenger of the gods, to the realm of Hel, the world of the dead, to try and bring Baldr back to the realm of the Aesir gods. Hermodr received good news: Hel was willing to return Baldr to the realm of the gods, but only if all the living had wept for the god's death and expressed their desire to see him return.

The gods were happy with this news, for Baldr was loved by all, and so everyone was summoned to confirm their desire to see him return. All confirmed their wish, except one giantess who lived in the mountains. Because of her, Baldr could not return, and the gods were very sad.

But it was not long before the gods discovered that the heartless giantess was actually Loki, disguised to prevent Baldr's return.

Loki had committed many evil deeds, but his latest had exceeded the gods' patience. In addition, the gods and Loki exchanged insults, with Loki accusing the gods of sexual and moral misconduct, the use of seiðr, and prejudice. All the Asgardians agreed: Loki must be punished.

Loki tried to escape the gods' wrath and hid near a lake where salmon swam. He took the form of a salmon and mixed with the fish to avoid being found by the gods.

But Odin, who had the ability to see the whole world from his throne, quickly discovered Loki's hiding place.

Loki knew the gods would try to catch him, so he tried to predict how they would do it. He knew that bait and a hook would be too simple for the gods, so he thought of something more elaborate.

Loki devised a braid of ropes that could form a net capable of catching fish. This tool became the world's first fishing net. Loki also devised some strategies for escaping.

When he saw the gods approaching, Loki threw the net into the fire and jumped back into the lake. The gods saw Loki jump into the water, but they didn't know how to catch him.

But the gods found traces of the net, which had not been completely burned, and understood the purpose of Loki's invention. So they made more nets and tried to catch the god of deception.

Loki tried every trick in the book to escape the nets the gods threw, sometimes jumping out of the water, but Thor had a brilliant idea. He realized that if a bear could catch a salmon in midair, so could he. When Loki leapt out of the water in the form of a fish, Thor was ready to catch him.

Loki was dragged by the gods into a cave to receive his deserved punishment. He was bound and imprisoned with the guts and sinews of his own son. The gods wanted to kill Loki for what he had done to Baldr, but Loki had made a blood pact with Odin. Despite their different origins, Loki and Odin considered themselves blood brothers, and Odin could not allow Loki to die. But simple imprisonment was too mild a punishment for the traitor.

Skadi decided to punish Loki for his evil deeds by taking a snake that secreted poisonous venom and tied it to a stalactite above Loki's head. When the snake began to drool, its venom fell on the god and caused him excruciating pain.

Loki had a faithful wife, Sigyn, who stayed by his side during the punishment. Sigyn tried to ease Loki's suffering by collecting the poison in a bowl. But over time, the bowl would fill up and Sigyn would have to leave to empty it. When this happened, the poison would return to Loki's skin, and he would scream in pain. The devoted wife would return to her place as quickly as possible and try once more to ease her husband's suffering. Every drop of venom that fell on Loki only increased his desire for revenge. So Loki vowed to repay the Asgardian gods for all the suffering they had caused him during Ragnarök.

The Great Battle of Ragnarök

The people of Midgard were descended from Askr and Embla, the first human couple created by the gods. They knew that they were protected by powerful deities who defended them from the forces of chaos.

Thor, known as the Slayer of the Giants, was always ready to protect the human world from any threat. Thanks to their protection, mankind thrived and always offered their gods the sacrifices they deserved.

The people of Midgard were used to facing life's difficulties, including the harshness of winter. But they knew that the realm of the gods would not last forever and that one day the Asgardian gods would have to face the forces of evil in Ragnarök.

It was the beginning of the end of summer, and everyone was expecting a great harvest, but suddenly a cold wind began to blow, and frost destroyed much of the crops.

The leaves of the trees quickly took on the colors of autumn and began to fall much earlier than expected, a sign that a harsh and long winter was coming. Despite the people's determination to prepare as best they could for the cold, it was impossible to be ready for the nightmare that was about to descend upon the earth.

So Fimbulvetr came, bringing three long winters with no summer in between. Men and animals sought refuge from the intense cold in their shelters, but the nights seemed endless. Every night, they feared that the sun would never rise again and that the frost would consume them.

They were running out of food, and the hunger forced them to eat anything they could find, even their pets. Those who risked going out to find other animals to slaughter became easy prey for the pack of Fenrir's children.

The situation worsened as the men began to fight each other for the few resources that remained. Brother against brother, sons challenging their fathers, war axes stained with blood. Chaos reigned, and humanity seemed to have forgotten the importance of unity and mutual aid.

Lack of food had forced many to cannibalism, and few men survived the endless winter.

Meanwhile, in Asgard, the Aesir saw that Ragnarök—the twilight of the gods—was approaching. The prophecy had come true, and chaos had reached the realm of men.

Two wolves, Hati and Skoll, who claimed to be the children of Fenrir, crossed the skies in pursuit of the sun and the moon. But despite their efforts to evade the wolves, the deities who represented the two stars could not escape forever. Eventually, the wolves reached their prey and devoured them, leaving the world in darkness.

Great earthquakes shook Yggdrasill, the World Tree, and cracks opened in the sky. The mountains collapsed, and the rock that held the wolf Fenrir was destroyed.

In addition, the colossal snake spat its venom, contaminating the water and killing everything from plankton to whales. It was a terrible moment for sea life.

At this critical moment, Loki, the God of Lies, was freed from his bonds and, like his son Fenrir, had only one desire in his heart: to destroy the gods of Asgard. He descended to Helheim, the realm where the souls of those who died unworthy went, and there his daughter Hel reigned.

The queen of the underworld, Hel, gave her father, Loki, command of an army of the undead, made up of the corpses of those who had died in dishonorable ways. These Norse zombies were eager to achieve the glory they had not received in life.

Níðhǫggr, the dragon who chewed the roots of the World Tree, dug a tunnel for the army of the dead to march into the land of men. Columns of fire signaled that the army of Muspelheim was marching, led by the mighty Surtr the Black, who burned everything in his path with his blazing sword.

The ice giants of Jotunheim boarded a ship to reach Vigridr, the place chosen as the battleground between the gods and the forces of chaos.

Heimdall, the herald of the gods, sounded the Gjallarhorn, and its blast was heard throughout the universe, announcing the beginning of the last great battle.

The forces of chaos, led by Loki, were eager to end the rule of the Asgardians and conquer them. The gods of Asgard knew this day would come and had prepared for it for millennia. The gates of Valhalla opened, and thousands of fearless warriors who had fought bravely throughout their lives emerged to form Odin's army.

These warriors had been taken by the Valkyries to the Valhalla hall, where they awaited the opportunity to show their courage again by fighting alongside the gods. All gods capable of wielding a weapon joined the fighters to face the forces of chaos and defend their kingdom.

The enormous army of the Muspelheim giants set out to conquer Asgard. However, an unexpected event changed everything: the Bifrost bridge collapsed and much of the army fell into the waters. The Asgardians celebrated their victory, but the gods knew that their fate was not to hide behind the powerful walls erected by the giant builder, but that they had to face the forces of darkness in the open field.

So, with the courageous Odin on his eight-legged horse, the army of the gods advanced towards the war front. The impact of the two armies was so strong that it made even Yggdrasill, the tree of worlds, tremble. The valiant Thor, the champion of the gods, was eager to face the giants and protect his people.

The ice giants faced the army of the gods with great courage, led by Loki and his armies of the undead of Hel. At the same time, the courageous Freyr, the Vanir god, rode his golden boar alongside the Asgardians, ready to challenge the powerful Surtr, the leader of the fire giants of Muspelheim.

Despite his commitment, Freyr was unable to defeat Surtr and fell on the battlefield, regretting having given Skirnir his magic sword. This event marked the beginning of the end for the gods, as many others would follow Freyr in death.

Even the brave Tyr, the warrior-god who sacrificed his hand to capture the wolf Fenrir., would fall on the battlefield, but not before plunging his sword into the heart of Garmr, the mighty wolf of Hel.

But the fighting did not end there. The battlefield shook as Jörmungandr, the fearsome World Serpent, entered the fray, spewing a cloud of poisonous gas that killed many of the gods' warriors. But Thor, the brave god of thunder, was thrilled at the sight of his old rival and couldn't wait to face him in a decisive battle.

The battle between Thor and Jörmungandr was an epic event that marked a significant moment. The giant serpent tried to devour the brave Thor, but with his wit and strength, he managed to dodge the blows and counterattack with his mighty hammer.

In the end, Thor was victorious, and the serpent fell wounded. The gods and warriors of Asgard rejoiced in their champion's victory, but unfortunately, Thor's blow was so powerful that it ruptured the serpent's poisonous sacs and spread a malevolent cloud around the god. Sadly, Thor fell to his knees and died of the poison.

Fenrir, Loki's son, devoured all who stood against him. But his true desire was to face Odin, the supreme god of Asgard, in an epic battle.

Unfortunately, Odin was not destined to emerge from this battle alive. In an act of bravery, Odin faced Fenrir, but the wolf opened its huge mouth and devoured the father of all gods. This event unleashed an uncontrollable rage in the heart of Widar, Odin's son, who decided to avenge his father's death.

Widar attacked Fenrir with surprising strength and managed to defeat him. By placing his feet on the wolf's tongue, his strong arms ripped out his teeth and split Fenrir's jaw in two, killing him.

Despite the death of his son, Loki was pleased to see the gods fall one by one. But his joy didn't last long, for Heimdall, guardian of the Rainbow Bridge, joined the fray and made his way toward Loki to face him in an epic duel.

The duel between Heimdall and Loki was a deadly dance of skill and mastery. Both warriors were wounded several times, but in the end, neither emerged victorious, as both died. The giant Surtr set the world on fire with his blazing sword, devouring everything in its path. There were no fighters left among the living or the giants; only ashes remained on the ground.

The flames also consumed Asgard and its great palaces, and the ocean rose, causing a great flood. The end of the era of the Asgardians had come.

Ragnarök's devastation left the world in a sea of water and darkness. But soon a new sun rose, bringing new life to the earth. Though the tree of Yggdrasill fell, the gods had prepared a special surprise. Hidden in the large ash tree was a mortal couple, Lif and Lifthrasir. Thanks to their love, the world was once again populated.

After the disappearance of the Asgard kingdom, a new kingdom called Idavoll took its place. Six gods were chosen to rule this new realm: Widar and Vali, sons of Odin; Magni and Modi, sons of Thor, who inherited his hammer; and Baldr and Hodr, resurrected from the world of the dead.

These new gods vowed not to repeat the mistakes of the past, remembered the old traditions, and discussed the future. They discovered the gold pieces used in the games of the gods and started a new game of the ancestral game. The kingdom of Idavoll flourished under their leadership, and a new cycle began.

CHAPTER 7
Mysteries of the North: Exploring the Curiosities of Norse Mythology

The Ends Times - The Religious Meaning of Ragnarök

Ragnarök, often referred to as the "Doom of the Gods" or the "Twilight of the Gods," is a concept that captivates the imagination with its grandeur and apocalyptic vision. It is not merely a tale of doom but a complex weave of themes that deeply resonate with the human experience.

At the very core of the Ragnarök narrative lies the intriguing idea of predestination. The gods—mighty, immortal beings—are fully aware of the ominous prophecies that foretell their own end. These events were preordained, their destiny spun long ago by the Norns. Yet, how do they respond? With extraordinary bravery, and it is this response that opens the door to a form of religious fatalism. Actions performed in the present are tinged with the immutable hues of future inevitability. However, let's not mistake this for nihilism; far from it. This awareness infuses life with meaningful urgency, a call to live honorably and courageously, fulfilling one's duties with integrity before the grand finale. It echoes the quintessentially Norse notion of "dying well," where one's character is measured by facing certain doom with valor.

Another captivating layer in this narrative is the promise of cyclical renewal. After the horrifying cataclysms cease, a reborn world will rise from the watery depths. This cyclical worldview reveals the Norse perception of time as a circle rather than a straight line. It offers reassuring existential comfort: the end is never really the end but a precursor to a new beginning.

Let's also consider the humility this tale imparts. The gods themselves are not eternal, omnipotent entities; they too are subject to the cosmic laws of change and decay. This perspective is deeply grounding, complicating our view of these gods by rendering them more relatable, bound by universal rules just as we are.

And here's a curiosity: our understanding of Ragnarök may very well be shaped by Christian influences. The Norse sagas were orally transmitted long before being written down, most likely after the advent of Christianity in the region. Therefore, the promise of renewal and resurrection may not have been original components of this tale.

In today's world, Ragnarök has found new life through the lenses of popular culture—cinema, video games, television series—all playing on the theme of rebirth following cataclysmic destruction. While the tale may outline the end of the world, it also carries within it the seeds of a brighter, more hopeful tomorrow. Quite a story to ponder upon, wouldn't you agree?

The Relationship between Human and Trees

Through the lush forests of Norse mythology, trees are not mere objects but veritable pillars connecting the realms of the living, the gods, and the cosmos. At the heart of this mystical relationship stands Yggdrasil. Unlike any ordinary tree, Yggdrasil serves as the axis mundi, a central point that ties together all realities. What is even more captivating is the notion that Yggdrasil possesses its own consciousness. This is not just a tree; it is a living entity that serves as a symbol of the intertwined destinies of humans and trees.

In ancient Scandinavia, surrounded by trees that were not merely part of the scenery but an integral aspect of life, ash and yew trees were highly esteemed. Ash trees were thought to share a kinship with Yggdrasil itself. Yew trees, on the other hand, often found their home in graveyards; their durable wood served as a material emblem of eternal life. While it's true that trees were crucial for practical needs such as constructing houses and ships, crafting tools, and providing fuel, their role extended far beyond the utilitarian.

Sacred groves were places believed to be inhabited by gods and were spaces where it was common to offer sacrifices and conduct religious rites. Areas within these groves were often cleared in honor of gods or goddesses, serving as the junction between the mortal and spiritual worlds. Many myths echo this sentiment, such as the story of Ask and Embla, the first humans, who were fashioned from ash and elm trees by Odin and his brothers, Vili and Ve.

For the Norse, trees were also oracles of wisdom. It was beneath the roots of Yggdrasil that Odin made an immense sacrifice, offering an eye to drink from Mímir's well and attain wisdom that knows no equal. The tradition of "Treespirit" further underscores the spiritual dimension of trees in this culture. Each tree was believed to house a spirit, which could be invoked for protection or prosperity. Rituals and offerings were common at the base of sacred oaks and ashes. Even the practice of rune-carving, usually done on wooden staves, contributed to the perception that trees were repositories of arcane knowledge.

The very physiology of Yggdrasil reflects cycles akin to those of human life and seasonal agriculture. Gnawed at by Níðhǫggr, the World Tree nevertheless endures, nourished by the Norns who water its roots. It's a cycle of perpetual decay and renewal, reflecting an understanding of ecological balance and the importance of stewardship. The tale of Ratatoskr, although not human, serves as a messenger between worlds, much like how trees function as mediums for rune reading and other divine consultations.

Now, let's turn our gaze to Ragnarök. Even in this scenario, Yggdrasil holds its ground. The tree trembles but does not fall. From its very trunk will emerge a man and a woman—Lif and Lifthrasir—to repopulate the earth. Trees, it seems, are not only the keepers of life but also of hope, even when faced with apocalyptic destruction.

So the Norse relationship with trees appears as a setting where the practical, the sacred, and the mystical are woven together seamlessly. Trees serve as providers, sanctuaries, and wisdom keepers. They offer us a worldview in which humans are intricately linked with nature, all anchored by the magnificent Yggdrasil.

The Enchantment of Steel - The Role of Magic Swords in Norse Mythology

Ah, if only these ancient blades could speak, what secrets and tales they would unfurl! Imagine walking through a world where swords are not just implements of battle, but also storied instruments of destiny, arcane knowledge, and cosmic power. Let's delve into this fascinating realm where swords transcend mere metal and craftsmanship to become entities of mystical significance.

Take, for instance, Gram, the illustrious sword wielded by the heroic Sigurd to vanquish the dragon Fafnir. This is no ordinary blade; it's a work of art, forged by the skillful dwarf Regin. Its edge is so sharp it could sever an anvil, and so delicate it could slice through floating wool. The sword becomes more than an accessory in Sigurd's narrative; it symbolizes not only his courage but also his destiny, leading him to battle a dragon who is not merely a beast but a transformed entity, intricately woven into the fabric of a much larger tale.

Then there's Tyrfing, a sword with a personality as dual as its craftsmanship, offering both blessings and curses. Forged by dwarves, the blade is haunted by an ominous rule: it must claim a life each time it is unsheathed. Here we have a powerful artifact that exemplifies the double-edged nature of power itself—grandiose yet laden with inherent risks, a conductor of fate that also entraps its wielder in an unpredictable web of consequences.

And let us not overlook Dáinsleif, a sword named after its dwarven creator, Dáin, which eventually finds its way into King Högni's arsenal. This blade comes with a frightful characteristic: wounds inflicted by it never heal, leaving its victims to suffer eternally. The sword emanates an aura of inevitability and irrevocable destiny, transforming it from a mere weapon into an object laden with ominous significance.

Of course, swords are not the exclusive domain of mortal heroes. Even the gods of Norse mythology possess magical weapons that share similar symbolic functions. Although Thor's Mjölnir is not a sword, its role parallels that of these enchanted blades in many ways. The hammer becomes an extension of Thor's divine authority to maintain cosmic order. Similarly, Odin's spear Gungnir, while not a sword, serves comparable metaphysical purposes, defining Odin's identity and cosmic role.

It's incredible how these swords even take on cosmic dimensions. The end times of Ragnarök see Surtr wielding a sword ablaze, its fire so luminous it overshadows the sun itself. In this apocalyptic moment, the sword symbolizes a terrifying power that marks the end of gods and men alike.

In the real world too, swords were considered more than just weapons. They were often included in burial rites, signifying their importance not only in life but also in the afterlife. Some were even cast into bodies of water as offerings to gods. Intriguingly, the inscriptions and patterns adorning these Viking swords were likely more than mere decoration; they were probably believed to imbue the blades with magical or protective qualities.

The Price of Power - Human Sacrifice in Norse Mythology

In a world where the gods seem to have an insatiable appetite for human blood, where the ultimate act of devotion involves hanging from a tree or being pierced by a spear, we are not discussing mere tales of horror. We are entering the mystical domain of Norse mythology, where human sacrifice was considered an essential component in maintaining cosmic balance.

Ah, yes, hanging. It's almost as if the air grows thicker just by uttering the word. In Norse mythology, this particular form of human sacrifice held a place of peculiar esteem. Odin had a particular penchant for this ritual. One would offer what became renowned as "Odin's Tree" or "Odin's Gallows," a gift so exalted it was believed to reside forever with the god, granting him eternal glory.

You may ask yourself, "Who would volunteer for such a gruesome fate?" Interestingly enough, candidates weren't exactly lining up. Those who found themselves hanging from trees were often criminals or captured enemies. But believe it or not, there were those courageous—or perhaps foolhardy—souls who volunteered, seeking to earn Odin's favor in the most radical way imaginable.

Then there is spear-stabbing, another form of offering a soul to the gods. Often executed in front of a statue or effigy of Odin, this ritual was believed to be a potent means to earn divine favor, especially during critical times—such as periods of war, crop failure, or natural calamities.

And Odin was hardly the sole recipient of these macabre gifts. Other gods like Thor and Freyja were also on the list of divine entities who received human sacrifices. But Odin, with his specific domains of war and death, was most intimately associated with this ritual, an act so severe it became the ultimate offering to the god.

In epochs past, such practices were not only accepted but also somewhat fashionable, a way to curry favor with the divine in times of need. Today, we can breathe a sigh of relief that such forms of devotion have been relegated to the annals of history. The rise of Christianity—though the latter was not exactly harmless—and the passage of time have ensured that human sacrifices have become stories of a distant past, a cautionary tale of what humanity should not return to.

When looking at these ancient practices, it's important to place them within their historical and cultural contexts, resisting the urge to judge them through a contemporary lens. Because who knows? Future generations might look back at some of our own practices and shake their heads in disbelief. Therefore, let us proceed with humility and caution, always aspiring to become the more enlightened beings we strive to be.

The Threads of Ancestry - The Interconnections Between Indo-European Myths and Norse Myths

At a crossroads where numerous paths diverge, each leading to a different enchanted realm of gods, heroes, and mythical tales, one might think these roads are disconnected at first glance. However, let's embark on a fascinating journey—akin to an archaeological dig through narratives—and you'll find that the paths are actually interwoven with threads of ancient myths and stories that span vast geographical landscapes.

Let's begin with the most rudimentary of connections: linguistic lineage. Old Norse, the language of the Vikings, is but one branch on the sprawling Indo-European linguistic family tree, whose roots stretch from the icy coasts of Scandinavia to the fertile plains of India. These ancient languages whispered the adventures of gods and heroes, and as they evolved, carried with them stories that, although morphing over time, share familial bonds.

Consider the characters who inhabit these myths. Take the archetype of the thunder god, for example. In the Norse realm, he manifests as Thor, the hammer-wielding protector of mankind. Journey to ancient India, and you'll find Indra, the Vedic god of rain and thunderstorms. These characters serve as molds, carved from similar heroic material. But the commonalities don't end there. Both traditions propose a cosmic order—Rta in the Vedic tradition and Orlog in the Norse—that maintains the balance of the universe.

Ah, the World Tree! A concept so vivid it appears as Yggdrasil in Norse mythology and the Ashvattha tree in Hindu cosmology. These are not mere trees; they are cosmic axes connecting the heavens, the earth, and the underworld—a sort of divine infrastructure, if you will.

Consider also the sacred animals. In the semi-legendary sagas of Norway, King Augvald venerates a sacred cow, which accompanies him wherever he travels and is believed to have the power to grant fertility and prosperity. Doesn't this echo the exalted status of cows in Hindu mythology?

The trickster figure, ah! Whether it's Loki in Norse myths, Varuna in Vedic tales, or even Hermes in Greek mythology, these characters add a pinch of chaos and unpredictability to the divine dramas, transcending regional limitations.

Now, on to heroes embarking on perilous quests. Whether it's Thor striving to reclaim his hammer Mjölnir, Vedic gods seeking immortality, or Greek heroes like Hercules overcoming incredible odds, this universal storyline transcends geographical and cultural boundaries.

The motif of twins or dualities is another shared theme. Norse mythology offers us Baldr and Hodr, or Freyr and Freyja, while Vedic tales provide the Ashvins, and Roman stories introduce Romulus and Remus. These dual figures often represent contrasting elements—light and darkness, life and death—showcasing the universal dual nature of existence.

In the concept of the afterlife, Norse mythology has the Hall of Valhalla, which awaits the bravest warriors judged by Odin himself. This is strikingly similar to the Greek Underworld presided over by Hades.

Finally, end-of-times myths like the Norse Ragnarök and the Hindu Kali Yuga tell us that the world, as we know it, is bound to end, giving way to a new beginning.

These complex myths, formed through centuries of cultural interactions and migrations, tell a shared story. It's a tale of common beginnings and diverse paths, of age-old questions and the human quest for the unknown.

Yet, the dialogues between these mythologies are not confined to a distant past. Their influence reverberates through time, even shaping contemporary interpretations and revivalist movements. Timeless myths continue to provoke thought and inspire the modern human spirit.

CHAPTER 8
The Influence of Norse Mythology on Our Lives Today

The fascinating universe is embedded in the very names of the days of the week! Let's uncover the amazing stories that lie behind something as simple yet profound as the names of the days.

Starting with Sunday—a day named after Sol, the radiant sun goddess. Can you imagine her majestically steering her chariot across the sky, led by two splendid horses? Ah, here comes the twist: Skoll, the monstrous wolf, trails behind her, nipping at her heels and occasionally biting hard enough to create what we call a solar eclipse.

Then we have Monday. The stage remains celestial, but this time it's Mani, the moon god, who is in the limelight. He, too, is on a chariot, scurrying across the night sky. But like Sol, he is not alone. Hati, another giant wolf, chases him. When the wolf gets close, a lunar eclipse occurs.

Onto Tuesday, or should we say, Tyr's Day? Tyr is the god with a challenging portfolio that encompasses, to say the least, both war and justice.

Wednesday—here's a little etymological trick—is named after none other than Odin himself, the god of many names. In Old English, he was known as Woden. And then Thursday! It's Thor's Day, named for the god of thunder, who wields his mighty hammer, Mjolnir.

Friday is quite unique. While it's named after Venus in the Roman tradition—a goddess of love, beauty, and fertility—in Norse mythology, it is known as Frigga's Star.

As for Saturday, it is named after Saturn, both the planet and the Roman god of agriculture. Interestingly, in Norse mythology, there is no direct match for Saturday, even though the Norse gods were no strangers to the themes of fertility and harvest.

But wait, there's more! Have you ever wondered where Yule logs, Christmas trees and even the act of decorating Easter eggs come from? The joys we find today have their roots in ancient Norse traditions.

Ah, Santa Claus and his reindeer flying across the night sky! Some believe this festive routine mimics the Wild Hunt of Norse mythology. During this event, people would leave a sack of hay for Sleipnir, Odin's exceptional eight-legged horse. Isn't it fascinating to think that this tradition has morphed into leaving cookies and milk out for Santa today?

So you see, the Vikings were far from being mere barbaric plunderers. They were carriers of traditions, values, and myths that have left an indelible mark on history and continue to resonate in the ways we understand our world today.

Shipbuilding and Seafaring

In ancient shipyards, you encounter the pinnacle of marine technology of the time—Viking longboats. These aren't mere boats; they are magnificent inventions, manifestations of a society's brilliance in seafaring and shipbuilding. The longboat is characterized by a shallow hull and a remarkable line of oars. This design is a product of refined engineering, aimed at achieving a unique blend of speed and agility on the high seas. Contrast these lightweight, agile vessels with the cumbersome, heavier ships of other cultures from the same period, and you'll begin to grasp the Vikings' tactical edge in naval endeavors.

But let's not forget the other pillar of Viking marine mastery: navigation. If their ships were the muscles, then navigation was the nervous system—a series of tools and techniques so advanced they would be considered revolutionary even today. Take, for example, the solar compass. Using calcite crystals, this instrument allowed the Vikings to pinpoint the sun's position even when it was hidden by clouds or had sunk below the horizon. Consider this—a way to find one's direction without the sun being visibly present! It's as if these seafarers possessed an ancient form of GPS, enabling them to traverse vast, uncharted waters with confidence.

These breakthroughs in shipbuilding and navigation laid the foundation for the nautical technologies that followed.

Language

The Vikings' impact on Britain extends beyond tales of violence and plunder. They traded goods, tilled soil, and even married locals. Yes, they were also settlers who deeply intermingled with the British population.

This human tapestry led many Norse tribes, predominantly from Scandinavia, to settle permanently in the British Isles. And here's the intriguing part: their language merged with the local tongue, laying the groundwork for modern English. Even today, words like "husband," "window," "sky," and "egg" bear the indelible imprint of Old Norse.

Literature

The enthralling power of Norse sagas and mythology has left an unforgettable footprint on the literary world. You may already know J.R.R. Tolkien, a luminary deeply enamored with these ancient Nordic narratives. One can easily sense their influence, rippling through his portrayals of elves, dwarves, dragons, and the majestic realms and cataclysmic battles that define his oeuvre.

Yet Tolkien is merely one star in a constellation of writers. From the grandiosity of Beowulf to contemporary fantasy epics, Norse legends continue to shape tales of heroism, mystical creatures, and awe-inspiring worlds. Truly, their influence seems to know no bounds, captivating the imaginations of readers for generations.

Trade and Economy

Let's ponder for a moment the remarkable contributions of the Vikings as economic pioneers. Yes, they reached as far afield as Dnepropetrovsk and even conducted trade with the Byzantine Empire, all while maintaining business ties with the Baltic states and the Franks. Can you imagine? These journeys also took them to places like China, India, the Middle East, and Russia, turning them into one of history's most cosmopolitan trading civilizations.

Consider this: would Dublin, that European gem, even exist in its current splendor were it not for Viking-founded trade routes? The Vikings not only founded cities but also established market towns and devised sophisticated systems of currency and barter, laying the essential groundwork for modern commerce. The economic landscape of the Middle Ages, and consequently today's world, owes much to their ventures.

Religion

The Vikings were a civilization deeply immersed in religious practices. Much like the legendary cultures of the Egyptians, Romans, Greeks, and Indians, the Vikings too had a whole pantheon of gods and goddesses they revered.

Now, here's a fascinating nugget: the Christmas tree tradition that we cherish today can actually be traced back to the Vikings. Yes, they venerated Yggdrasil, an ash tree considered sacred and a cosmic axis holding the Nine Realms together. This tree wasn't just any tree; it symbolized life, renewal, and hope. And this Viking tradition—believe it or not—has trickled down through history to become an integral part of our Christmas festivities today.

Norse Mythology and Popular Culture

Who doesn't love a good old-fashioned superhero story? When it comes to Norse gods, Thor and the Avengers have certainly made a significant impact on popular culture. However, don't forget that the legends of the Aesir gods have been thrilling audiences for centuries before they hit the big screen.

From ancient poetry to modern art, the stories of Odin, Thor, and the rest of the gang have captured the imaginations of generations. If you're looking for a deeper understanding of Norse mythology's influence on popular culture, buckle up, as we're about to explore some fascinating perspectives.

Books

G.K. Chesterton's "The Ballad of the White Horse" (1911) may turn your world upside down. It portrays the Norse gods as false gods and aims to convert the reader to Christianity. While it offers an interesting take on the gods from a Christian perspective, it's crucial to remember that all perspectives come with their own biases. Even if the book challenges your beliefs, it remains an entertaining read. Who knows, it might even deepen your appreciation for Snorri Sturluson's "Poetic or Prose Edda."

L. Sprague de Camp's "The Incomplete Enchanter" (1941) is far from incomplete when it comes to enchanting its readers. Just three decades after Chesterton's interpretation of the Norse gods, de Camp offers a much more exciting version. The gods in this literary series are a feast for the imagination, brimming with rich detail and larger-than-life personalities. They instill a sense of wonder and awe, reminding you of the power of dreams and the primal instincts that exist in all of us.

J.R.R. Tolkien's "The Hobbit" (1937) and "The Lord of the Rings" (1954) are two of the most iconic books of our time, undoubtedly influenced by the Norse gods and the realms of Yggdrasil. From the wise and powerful Gandalf, who bears a striking resemblance to Odin, to the elves and dwarves who capture the essence of Norse mythology.

Douglas Adams' "Life, the Universe, and Everything" (1982) will take you on a fantastic journey through alternate worlds, beliefs, and adventures featuring Odin and Thor. This blend of science fiction and myth will keep you on the edge of your seat, eager to discover what's around the next corner. From fantastic worlds to mind-bending theories, this book offers an epic tale that combines the best elements of science fiction and mythology.

Poetry

William Morris, a virtuoso in the world of poetry, offers Norse mythology-inspired masterpieces like "Sigurd the Volsung," which serve as conduits to an otherworldly realm of mythical beings and grand conflicts.

If your literary appetite seeks a seminal Norse-inspired work revitalized with flair, you simply can't overlook Seamus Heaney's "Beowulf." Heaney's rendition is a tour de force that reanimates this ancient tale. While retaining its authentic core, he enriches it with contemporary nuances, making it an essential read.

Music and Song

Richard Wagner, the brilliant German composer, gave birth to the monumental "Der Ring des Nibelungen," a quartet of operas rooted in Norse figures. These operas serve as portals to an ethereal realm, graced with mythical beings and indelible melodies.

For those whose tastes veer toward the intensity of heavy metal, groups like Manowar, Unleashed, and Kampfar are your go-to options. They amplify the vigor of Norse myths, delivering it directly to your soul through electrifying compositions and potent lyrics.

Movies

Let's start with the monumental "Vikings" series from The History Channel. This sweeping narrative immerses you in the universe of the great Norse warriors, replete with divine interventions, audacious battles, and thrilling voyages.

For Marvel enthusiasts, Thor and his group of Avengers provide adrenaline-fueled exploits. These cinematic gems will capture your attention as you accompany our heroes on their globe-saving endeavors.

If it's laughter you seek, "Erik the Viking" is your ticket. This comedy offers a lighthearted spin on Norse lore, certain to keep you chuckling.

And let's not overlook "The Thirteenth Warrior," an enthralling narrative of human courage and riveting adventure. With so many facets and layers to explore, each movie offers its own unique take on Viking and Norse mythology.

Other

The mesmerizing allure of Norse mythology indeed perpetually echoes through the corridors of our modern popular culture. Whether in the illustrated panels of comic books or the intricate worlds of video games like God of War, its presence is both undeniable and evergreen. As if awakening from the deep slumber of Ragnarök, these ancient tales resurface with newfound vigor, refusing to be confined to a single form of expression. It's as if the gods themselves wish for their stories to be eternally recounted, capturing the imagination of each succeeding generation.

CHAPTER 9
The History of Ásatrú

The tale of Ásatrú—so ancient and yet astonishingly resilient—paints a vivid picture. It's a belief system deeply rooted in the consciousness of Germanic people, almost erased from history as Christianity swept through the lands, converting souls as though gathering a harvest. However, Ásatrú was not to be consigned to oblivion. The 1970s marked a period redolent with the scent of mead and honey, as this age-old faith awakened from its long slumber.

In Iceland, precisely on the summer solstice of 1972, the "Íslenska Ásatrúarfélagið" emerged—a name even challenging for the most linguistically gifted among us. This fellowship acted as the catalyst that propelled Ásatrú back into the living world. Not to be outdone, the United States soon gave birth to its own movement with the formation of the Ásatrú Free Assembly, later rebranded as the Ásatrú Folk Assembly. One could almost hear the strumming of ancient lyres and see the flickering dance of bonfire flames.

What we are witnessing is not merely a European phenomenon. Through concerted global efforts, Ásatrú has been given a fresh chapter in its long narrative. For over a quarter of a century, the Ásatrú Alliance has celebrated its faith by holding an annual gathering known as "The Althing"—a vibrant communion where followers unite, sharing both lore and spirit.

How faithful are modern Ásatrú practices to those of their forebears? Remarkably so. The modern followers of this faith are like time travelers, meticulously recreating the rituals and beliefs of their ancestors. The result is an amalgam that blends the wisdom of ancient traditions with the nuances of contemporary culture, creating a compelling tapestry that resonates deeply with its adherents.

As for their source of wisdom, the Norse Eddas stand as the bedrock. These texts serve as a cornerstone, a near-biblical repository of knowledge—albeit one sadly diminished by Christian scrutiny that labeled these pagan practices as barbaric. Nonetheless, Ásatrú is also enriched by an unbroken line of folktales—stories handed down through the ages like the most delicate and meaningful game of telephone ever played. It's storytelling at its finest, an eternal loop of tradition and belief.

Before Christianity, the Ásatrú religion resembled the ancient ways of Norse culture, where gods walked the earth as living, breathing entities. This realm is not confined to the pages of comic books; it constitutes the very core of Ásatrú—a faith that views its divine beings less as ethereal spirits and more as superheroes, adorned with beards rather than spandex.

The pantheon of Ásatrú is organized with meticulous precision, akin to various departments in a vast celestial corporation. There are the Aesir, the primary objects of veneration, flanked by the Vanir and the Jotnar. Each group plays a unique yet interconnected role in this divine assembly.

Is there a moral compass to navigate this intriguing world? Absolutely. Enter the Nine Noble Virtues, the very tenets that could be likened to a Viking-era manifesto for living an exemplary life. Nine is a number that holds special allure in Norse cosmology, resonating through myths and legends. These virtues—ranging from courage to fidelity—are the keystones that fortify the Ásatrúar lifestyle.

The term "Ásatrú" itself is an etymological gem. While one might think it ancient, it actually derives from the Danish word "Asetro," a word that translates to "belief in gods," succinctly articulating the essence of the religion.

Consider this: Ásatrú claims an antiquity that rivals, or perhaps even surpasses, that of many established religions like Christianity and Buddhism. It is an awe-inspiring amalgamation of age-old features—some stretching back to the shamanistic practices of the Paleolithic era—alongside Neolithic sensibilities revolving around notions like "honor" and "shame." One might view it as a spiritual time capsule, conveyed through millennia.

Now, turn your gaze toward Iceland, a landscape where Ásatrú once flourished but was supplanted by Christianity. When settlers returned from European shores with Christian beliefs, the tension in Iceland escalated into what can only be described as a celestial tug-of-war. Eventually, to prevent societal splintering, a decision was made to unify the nation under the banner of Christianity.

Yet, like a phoenix rising from the ashes, Ásatrú has returned to the modern world. No longer a sidelined player, it has ascended as one of the most rapidly expanding faiths in Iceland today. Indeed, it represents a spiritual resurrection that could be considered one of the most spellbinding comeback stories of our times.

Let us delve deeper into the intriguing complexities of Ásatrú's beliefs, which stand in stark contrast to the monotheistic tenets of Abrahamic faiths. Imagine a spiritual realm where multiple gods are not only venerated but where the divine beings of other religions are also acknowledged. This setting is like a religiously inclusive social circle, accepting of diverse spiritual outlooks. It is vastly different from Christianity, which worships a singular God manifested in a Trinity, or Islam, which devoutly affirms the singularity of Allah while denying the validity of other religious perspectives.

However, not everyone who claims to adhere to Ásatrú truly understands its core philosophy. Unfortunately, there are individuals who have exploited this venerable faith to serve odious agendas, such as white supremacists who have distorted Ásatrú's teachings to propel their hateful ideologies. It is crucial to understand that Ásatrú was rekindled not as a vehicle for supremacy but rather as a means for Europeans to reestablish a link to their ancestral past.

Contrary to the false narratives espoused by such extremist groups, the majority of Ásatrúars are individuals seeking a deeper spiritual connection—nothing more, nothing less. To put it even more clearly, this is not a belief system exclusive to individuals of European descent; it particularly resonates with those whose ancestry is steeped in pagan traditions.

Therefore, one should not be misled by those who misuse Ásatrú for their narrow objectives. The faith's genuine adherents do not advocate for the domination of one group over another. Instead, the essence of Ásatrú rests on the pursuit of balance and harmony in life's multifaceted dimensions.

The Values of Norse Paganism

The backbone of this ancient belief system rests on unwavering loyalty to the Aesir and Vanir, the divine entities revered as our primordial relatives. Paying them homage is not a mere formality; it's an existential imperative, guided by the luminous compass of the Nine Virtues.

These Nine Virtues are not mere ethical bullet points. Far from it. Think of them as a recipe for an enlightened existence, harmonizing not just our relationship with deities, but also with the Earth and our fellow humans. By embracing these principles, we step closer to the gods, earning their admiration and perhaps also the regard of our ancestors.

Nine Virtues

Courage

Courage is often lauded as the sovereign among virtues. Let's dispel a myth: courage is not confined to battlefield heroics. In today's nuanced world, courage transforms into moral bravery—the audacity to uphold what's just, even when society may disagree. Standing up for one's convictions is a courageous act, isn't it? The realm of Ásatrú offers a splendid training ground to cultivate such moral courage, a virtue interwoven into the practice of all the other noble virtues.

Truth

The principle of truth demands more than mere honesty; it insists on the courage to voice that truth. Ah, the allure of the little white lie—how often it tempts us! Yet in the Ásatrú faith, lying is a marker of cowardice, a departure from the virtue of courage. The focus is on uncompromising adherence to our beliefs, even when the world would prefer we bend the truth. But what about those instances where deceit confronts us? Here, Norse wisdom lends subtlety: dishonesty is permissible only if it shields our honor, and even then, our motives must pass the litmus test of our own intentions.

Honor

Honor is not bland obedience to societal norms; it's a profound alignment with one's intrinsic moral code. Without this elemental virtue, the other virtues lack substance and meaning. Honor should be the internal arbiter in your decision-making process, helping you discern right from wrong. It is the guardian of your reputation, the custodian of your self-respect. Here is something often overlooked: to win the esteem of others, the first step is to honor oneself.

Fidelity

Fidelity is a virtue not confined to amorous relations, but one that extends across all aspects of life. Imagine fidelity as the golden thread weaving through our relationships—with deities, ideologies, loved ones, and even the person we see in the mirror. In the world of Ásatrú, fidelity is a non-negotiable tenet, a towering pinnacle in our moral landscape that makes us unyielding defenders of all that is sacred to us.

Discipline

Discipline, specifically the art of self-discipline, acts as the alchemical element fusing all virtues into a cohesive whole. This quality endows us with the fortitude to uphold our convictions and navigate life's labyrinth of choices, especially when those decisions are anything but easy. The wonder of self-discipline lies in its malleability—it is a skill under our absolute control, honed through sheer will and tenacity. Who knows? Fortifying this virtue might reveal dormant capabilities, surprising even yourself.

Hospitality

Hospitality is a word that echoes through time, as resonant today as it was in the Old Norse era. The Ásatrú ethos places immense value on this virtue, urging us to extend kindness indiscriminately. After all, you never know—the stranger to whom you're being rude might be a god in disguise! Therefore, let's make it a practice to meet every interaction, whether in our homes or daily comings and goings, with the grace and openness one would offer to divine visitors.

Self-Reliance

Self-reliance is not a call for stubborn independence, but rather an appeal for judicious autonomy, balanced against the wisdom of collective guidance. If we cannot sustain ourselves, how can we aspire to uplift those around us? Escaping the snare of materialism becomes easier when we cultivate self-reliance. Indeed, the Norse people had inherent wisdom: they prized possessions for their functional merits, not merely for their material worth.

As you walk the Ásatrú path and strive for self-reliance, remember: if ever you stumble, the community of like-minded souls is never far and always ready to extend a supportive hand.

Industriousness

Industriousness—a virtue that would have been the talk of Valhalla—is a simple but potent concept. If an endeavor is worth our time and belief, then it commands our utmost effort. In the lexicon of Norse Paganism, 'laziness' finds no home. Therefore, let us aim sky-high, far beyond the confines of mediocrity. Every task at hand should not merely be done, but should be executed with an almost reverent pride, as if the gods themselves were watching.

Perseverance

Perseverance is the ability to dance in the rain, not just wait for the storm to pass. Life is an intricate tapestry of challenges, and at times, our aspirations may feel tantalizingly elusive. It is here that perseverance serves as our compass, guiding us through rough terrain and helping us rise each time we falter—wiser and fortified. Perseverance not only propels us individually, it magnifies its impact when embraced by an entire community. Together, under its umbrella, we can forge a collective that thrives on mutual betterment.

Norse Festivals and Rituals

Let's explore the celebratory aspects of Ásatrú—the festivals and rituals that add color to belief. In ancient Norse society, time was divided into a simple binary: summer and winter. The Spring Equinox welcomes summer with the Festival of Ostara, while the advent of winter is heralded by the Festival of Winter Nights following the Autumn Equinox. Celebrated either within local communities or on a grand national stage, these occasions are the pillars of Ásatrú festivities.

The calendar is filled with other joyous milestones, from elaborate Yule celebrations to intimate family gatherings. Some traditions maintain the ancient custom of small sacrifices, while others have evolved into harmonious assemblies centered around shared meals. Either way, in the world of Ásatrú, there is seldom a moment devoid of something worth celebrating.

Yule

Yule, a festival that envelops us in its magic from December 20, signifies a profound cosmic pivot. This moment marks the cessation of the year's deepest darkness and heralds the coming light, promising rebirth. Folklore tells us that this is when Baldr makes his return from Hel, easing winter's icy grip on the earth's surface. Over the course of 12 spirited nights, the celebration is replete with sumptuous feasts, melodious tunes, and the exchange of gifts. The term "Yule" traces its roots to the Old Norse word "HJOL," symbolizing the wheel of the year at its nadir, poised to ascend anew.

Disting
Fast forward to February 2, and we encounter Disting, a festival that delves into the reverence for female ancestral spirits and familial matrons, who are believed to still watch over their descendants with the help of Frigga. While the day may evoke the harshness of snow and cold, it also exudes an aura of healing. Ásatrú congregations gather, often around a warm hearth, sharing songs and extending spiritual comfort. A veritable epitome of unity, Disting celebrates the nexus between the divine and the familial.

Midsummer
As June 20 approaches, the Midsummer Blot makes its presence felt. This is the Summer Solstice, encapsulating the sun's zenith in a mere 48-hour span. Events during this holiday are far from sparse; they range from forging alliances to celebrating triumphant excursions in hunting and fishing. Midsummer offers not just an occasion to soak in the brilliance of the longest day but also serves as a reminder that challenges loom with the shortening days ahead. Thus, whether it's forming new bonds, acknowledging our achievements, or simply basking in solar splendor, Midsummer coaxes us to gather and celebrate the cornucopia of life's gifts.

Lithasblot
As July sets and August awakens, specifically between July 31 and August 1, Lithasblot unfurls its festive tapestry in homage to Freyr, the fertility god whose enchantments grace our fields with abundance. This period is rich in rituals, including the act of binding and blessing the first sheaf, an earthly tribute to heavenly beings. Wells and springs, nature's life sources, are adorned in a manner that resonates with ancient practices. The art of breaking bread assumes divine dimensions: loaves carved in the shape of Freyr are torn apart and distributed among the community as a sacrament of thanksgiving.

Mabon
As autumn's golden hues herald the onset of late September, Mabon—or Haustblot, as it's less commonly known—occupies a quieter but no less meaningful corner of the calendar. The date, around September 22, signifies the closing act of the harvest, a hectic period that allows for little pomp but abounds in purpose. Brief yet heartfelt feasts are dedicated to a pantheon of harvest gods, including Freyr, Nerthus, Iduna, and Njord. Special nods are given to Jord for her boundless bounty and to Snotra, who embodies hard work and hospitality. The guardianship of livestock, personified by Huldra, is acknowledged for securing the community's sustenance through the winter ahead.

Winter Nights
As October concludes and November dawns, the period between October 29 and November 1, Winter Nights burst forth in exultant pageantry, becoming an

arena where ancestral spirits are venerated and consulted for wisdom. These few days are considered a crucible for divining one's future. But what role do animals play in this? Certain creatures, lacking the vitality to endure winter's grasp, are sacrificed. This rite serves both pragmatic and spiritual ends, fortifying the community and dispelling malevolent forces. The duty is often carried out by the family's matriarch, who is seen as the custodian of domestic well-being. Through her invocations, she casts a protective mantle over her household, safeguarding its tranquility.

CONCLUSION

As we stand at the terminus of this captivating journey through the realms of Norse mythology, the time has come to say our farewells. I hope you have enjoyed exploring Viking culture, their beliefs, gods, goddesses, heroes, and creatures that make up this rich and fascinating tradition.

But this is far more than a mere anthology of myths and legends. Norse mythology is a living tradition, pulsating through time and leaving its indelible mark on art, literature, and even modern pop culture. On one side are the ancient sagas of the Eddas, and on the other, the colorful frames of Marvel Comics, all connected by the same narrative thread.

You, our companion on this wondrous journey, are the reason this work has been so deeply gratifying. Sharing this treasure trove of myths and lore with you has been nothing short of a labor of love, made all the more fulfilling by your keen interest and vibrant enthusiasm.

And now, we must part ways. As you leave, may the breezes of Valhalla guide you gently back to the world of mortals. May these sagas of gods and heroes fuel your imagination and bring you joy for countless seasons yet to come.

Until we meet again, a heartfelt Skål to you!

Dear Reader...

Our literary adventure has come to an end, at least for this book... Writing the manual you are holding in your hands has been a wonderful opportunity to challenge ourselves and open our hearts. We have put down on paper all our passion and experience gained in this field...

We hope that our company has intrigued and informed you, and that you have found useful insights and tools in the previous pages to develop your curiosity and passion for Norse Mythology and, as a result, to grow as a person and embody the values that make you unique and incomparable. Don't rush your learning; this is a journey that requires a lot of practice and commitment, but it should not stop you from achieving your goals.

Remember, the secret to an exciting and fulfilling life is to enjoy the journey.

If this is the case for you and you have found this book useful in any way, it would be fantastic if you could leave sincere feedback on Amazon to help us grow and spread our message to as many people as possible. We wish you all the best and have a good life!

<u>Scan below to leave a review for this book</u>

Greetings,

Inkwell House Press

**SCAN THE
QR CODE
TO DOWNLOAD
YOUR BONUS**

Printed in Great Britain
by Amazon

4805b9e2-f06c-4d9d-82e9-9b7d6aff3219R01